THE ART OF FORGIVENESS

SHORT FICTION

THE ART OF FORGIVENESS

SHORT FICTION

Chris Benjamin

GALLEON

The Art of Forgiveness

First Galleon Edition, July 2024
ISBN 978-1-998122-10-3

Published by Galleon Books
Moncton, New Brunswick, Canada
www.galleonbooks.ca

Cover image by Chris Benjamin.

"Operation Niblet" previously appeared in *Boy with a Problem* and is reprinted with permission from Pottersifled Press.

Library and Archives Canada Cataloguing in Publication

Title: The art of forgiveness : short fiction / Chris Benjamin.
Names: Benjamin, Chris, 1975- author
Identifiers: Canadiana 2024042879X | ISBN 9781998122103 (softcover)
Subjects: LCGFT: Short stories.
Classification: LCC PS8603.E5578 A89 2024 | DDC

C813/.6—dc23

GERRY

LONG

DREW

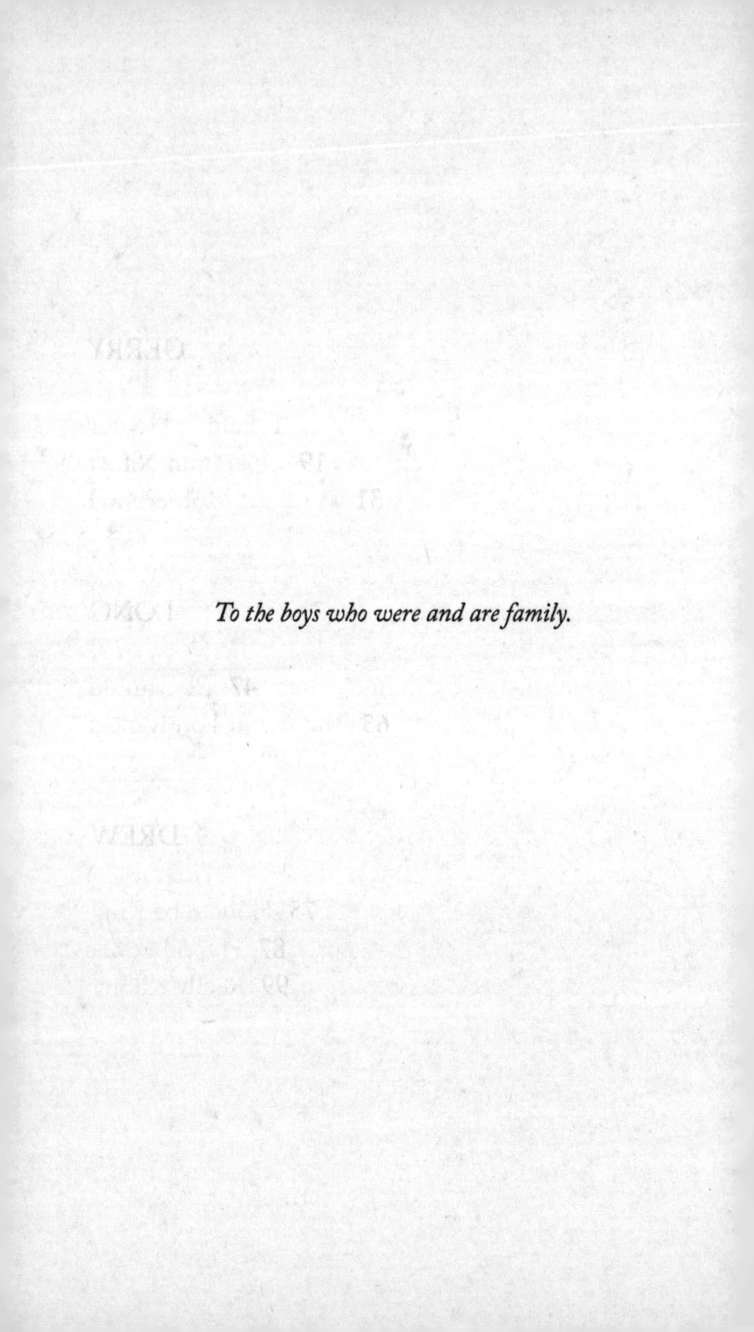

To the boys who were and are family.

GERRY

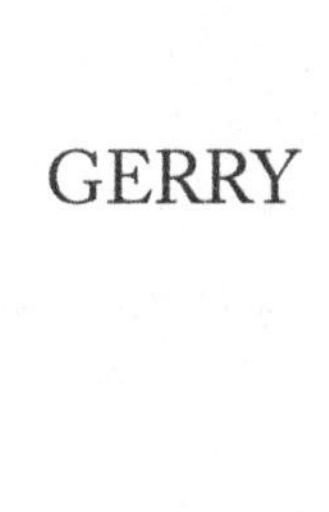

SAFE AS HOUSES

A DISCORDANT CHOIR of fan-club voices spiked the high tone submerging Gerry's head. Louder, more disjointed, the echo of echoes in a deep-sea cave. Gerry looked up to see Shaughnessy, his pro-wrestler physique hovering over him, splattered with blood. Two other boys in hoodies, track pants, high-tops and ball caps surrounded Shaughnessy, their shoulders heaving. They were Jason, who was Shaughnessy's younger brother, and Khrys. At that moment, Gerry found it difficult to tell them apart. The phrase *boy band gang* came to mind, a breakdance routine with kick steps to his face.

"Thank god he's conscious. I almost called his dad. Dude, that punch was badass."

Gerry heaved himself up but didn't make it. The ringing in his head choke-slammed him down again. He squinted at the light bulb hanging by a rope or a wire—it was hard to tell, from Shaughnessy's basement ceiling. Shaughnessy leaned on Khrys and shook his head, asked Gerry if he was sure he was not dead. Gerry spit on the concrete floor, told Shaughnessy to fuck himself. Tough like that. But he couldn't hear himself say it. The ringing overrode the sound of his voice. He only heard the others.

Shaughnessy leaned close and whispered, "Quit or keep goin'?"

Gerry nodded. "Fuck it."

Shaughnessy announced it, "Gerry says fuck it!" The fight was over.

Shaughnessy reached a gloved hand down and they linked arms at the elbow so Shaughnessy could pull him up. Sportsmanlike. Then he surprised Gerry with a bear hug, said it was a good effort.

"That my blood?"

Shaughnessy looked at Gerry's stomach and Khrys said, "Oh, shit."

The ringing pulled Gerry underwater again. He fought the current, stayed upright, asked someone, anyone, to help get his gloves off so he could stop the bleeding. Jason pulled him back with a rough shoulder massage that made Khrys laugh more. Jason, who like his brother knew boxing because their dad taught them, said chill, nosebleeds are normal. He put a rag that smelled like oil over Gerry's face, squeezed.

Gerry shrieked, drowning Jason's instructions to tilt his head down. "God fucking damn, it hurts."

"Something's broken," Jason said to Gerry as he unlaced his gloves.

Gerry was going to marry Mariah Cary. Jennifer

Mackay didn't know it yet. That was good, because although Jennifer Mackay was friends with all the right kids and was on the principal's Gold List and made oversized '70s sunglasses look cool, she talked to him all the time about random things, always asking him questions about what video games he was into or if he had seen any good movies lately. Also, importantly, she promised to show Gerry her boobs. In class he had jokingly asked if she could give him a picture of her posing like the "sunshine girl" in the *Toronto Sun*, which Khrys's father had brought home from a business trip. Jennifer refused, but she whispered to Gerry at lunch hour that for 50 bucks she'd give him a live glimpse, one Mississippi. If he told a soul, she'd fillet him. Jennifer's father was a doctor and her mother was a high school principal. They skied in Colorado for Christmas and spent March break in Florida. She captained their junior-high girls' volleyball team and the model UN.

Gerry lived in the smallest house in the subdivision, delivered newspapers for spending money, and his single dad was an office assistant. There was no doubting Jennifer's power to destroy him. He liked that they'd have a secret. He only cared a little whether anyone else had seen her boobs. He somewhat hoped he would be the first and, in his fantasies, she let him touch their firm softness and ever-so-briefly kiss her lips, too.

Trudging through snow, delivering newspapers in

the subdivision, he felt like the last of his kind. The subdivision must have had the highest per-capita rate of old timers and traditionalists in the world; they liked seeing a young man unafraid of hard work and most of them were generous tippers. Maybe they knew he was saving for a car, so he could get the fuck into town someday, when he turned 16. Maybe hit Neptune. His mother, when in certain softer moods, sometimes took him to see plays there. She always wanted to expose him to culture. Maybe his customers simply liked him that much. Maybe they felt bad for the half-orphan. Maybe they wanted him gone.

The ringing came and went. It left him at Blossom Lane and he was relieved. It was back by the time he got to #21, Ian Zhao's house. Ian was the white adopted son of Chinese parents. Their house looked like everyone else's, except for the picture lettering under the house number. Gerry had hoped it translated to something cool, like "power" or "strength," but when he asked Ian about it he'd raised an eyebrow and told Gerry no—it was just their house number in Chinese.

Gerry would have liked to get Ian Zhao into Shaughnessy's basement, wearing a pair of boxing gloves. Ian Zhao, hockey superstar, short and stupid and adopted, yet he made out with Jennifer. Gerry heard about it later. It happened at her birthday party, which Gerry did not attend, because he was not invited. Gerry made a wet snowball. The six inches that fell that morning had turned slushy. The #21, plus the Chinese symbols underneath, made an easy target. He missed, hit the picture window with a low reverb, *thwumm*. Mr. and Mrs. Zhou didn't get home till late. They had the kinds of jobs that left Ian to do whatever he wanted after school. Mostly he was out back practicing slap shots.

The ringing was pissing Gerry right off.

Gerry loved boxing, but he shouldn't have fought Shaughnessy. Shaughnessy was a statue sculpted from that meteoric material harder than diamonds. Gerry had never noticed it before, under Shaughnessy's Rick Astley face and faux-wet locks. So pretty. Gerry felt pretty stupid, thinking he had a chance against a guy that big, a gifted, all-around athlete with a known penchant for inflicting pain on lesser beings—from pulling the wings off bees when he was little to giving younger kids wedgies and snapping the bras of girls at school. Psychopath. But Gerry liked it at Shaughnessy and Jason's house, safely away from his father.

Gerry took his time with the day's route. He savoured the anticipation. The fear. In his dreams, one of Jennifer's boobs ambushed him with the promise of delight, delight which was putrefied when she forced him to bite it. It tasted and felt like last year's all-too-real periapical abscessed tooth. A wisecrack, a crack back from Father, and a "oh damn, sorry Gerald." As if his scarred fist had just slipped. As if it would never happen again. Gerry woke from this dream waiting for the good part, the release from dread.

He cursed his low pain tolerance. Always fighting the urge to whimper. Refusing to be the wimp his father assumed he was.

Gerry was afraid Jennifer wouldn't follow through. He was afraid her parents would be home early. He was also afraid she would follow through, and he couldn't quite disentangle the two. So he took his time, noticing the things he saw every day. He watched the crack in the asphalt running all the way uphill, wrinkles sprouting from it, like those on his mother's face when she ranted or laughed. She had a hard, hyperbolic laugh that Gerry always wanted to emulate because it seemed to be her most vicious offense against his father.

Gerry noticed the sameness of the houses. He'd never seen that before. He never thought they were alike. But now he noticed how each had a high side and a low side and a peaked roof, usually in the middle and sometimes off to the side. On one end, a picture window; on the other, two smaller windows. Some of the houses were bigger versions of the same, with an added floor and two-door garage.

He'd been living in the same neighrbourhood for six years and never given it much thought. In the version of this house where he'd lived with his father since his mother departed, the smallest version, Gerry wished for a bigger room, his own bathroom and shower, as separate as he could imagine from his father. Perhaps even a separate apartment to himself.

His dad said the subdivision was slapped together with whatever was left lying around, built in the 1970s, all by the same guy. When you threw in the pastels—pale yellow, salmon-peach, light blue, and middle-grade blue—it was amazing how many different looks the designer got out of that one look. You had to observe closely to avoid the feeling of floating between the lines of a page.

Gerry's dad had once said that the neighbourhood felt like "oblivion sliced in half." A semi-highway cut through the middle of the 'burb, and it was walled in by a ring road. The high-wail Doppler of the cars was a constant reminder that there was somewhere more important to go.

Even without the colours and patterns and house numbers, Gerry would still know one house from another. The owners broadcast themselves with distinctive decorations—the Zhous' Chinese characters, for example. The Chiassons with their tin Acadian star. The interlock walkway the MacGillivrays laid down every day of one sweat-soaked summer, now buckled by frost heaves. Mrs. Salah and her homemade prayer flags, cut into triangles from striped corduroy bolts she bought on a Lithuanian vacation with her ex. They pinwheeled around the thin string tying them across the frame of her front porch. The Grahams had the faces of smiling old men tacked into their tree trunks, made of spray-painted dollar-store craft plastic. Mr. DeLorey, who revered the trees as mystical harbingers of the eternal and would never penetrate their bark skin, hung Coke bottles from their branches with candles burning inside. They punctured the early dark of winter days.

Gerry had an erection observing these nearly identical, except not at all, houses. The ringing faded as he mechanically pulled each paper from his canvas bag, shoved them behind the screen doors and didn't think about Jennifer except thought of nothing else.

—

The first time Gerry boxed, in a windmill arc he forgot everything Jason had tried to show him—he neglected to keep Khrys away with the jab, didn't use his long skinny arms to create space or keep his elbows down fists high. His fist sailed past Khrys's ear and Khrys missed with a responding uppercut, Shaughnessy and Jason's laughter the backdrop. Swish, swish, nothing—but the arc of it sated, spiced with a vision of his father's sneer at the receiving end of it, obliterated. It was a haymaker on behalf of Mother, who had laughed herself to death watching stand-up on television at her friend Crystal's place. The doctors called it a ruptured brain aneurysm, an infarction of the medulla oblongata. Brain stem.

Gerry shoved Khrys into the plywood post and twisted yellow polypropylene rope around him—the post that Jason's father, a real boxer and carpenter, had constructed. Khrys didn't bounce back. He sagged and reached to the back of his head with a "Hey, hey, what the—" Gerry brought the rain, painted lightning across Khrys's right eye, darkened his brown upper cheek, split his lip with a left hook. Khrys, who abided no enemies, ceded the fight, called Gerry psycho. Khrys's smile made the whole basement feel warm.

Gerry lifted spent arms in a glorious V—it was everything Jason had promised when he'd invited Gerry over after school, saying, "Yeah, it hurts but it makes you feel frigging alive man, like real-life alive. Not just a video game." The implication was clear enough. They liked him enough to want to save him from his less cool friends of too much weight or too heavy an accent or who preferred their battles on a screen. What did Jason know? Until then, Gerry had had three close friends, but he'd drifted from all of them lately. High school was a different beast. He'd shrugged at Jason and said, "Whatever, sure." Better to get beat by a couple of assholes his own age than beat by his old man. Now he was smiling like an ecstatic minion at Shaughnessy, for some reason needing the big psycho's approval for the victory to count.

He didn't get it. "You two fight like beagles," Shaughnessy said.

—

Gerry didn't mention the ringing in his head to his friend, Grif—a kid a year younger than him, at one time his third best friend, who lived next to Jennifer. Grif's house was the penultimate house on his newspaper delivery route. Gerry was afraid that if he mentioned his recent hearing troubles, Grif would try to stop him from going back to his new friends' house. Grif hated Khrys, Jason, and especially Shaughnessy.

Grif lived with his nan. She was another of those adults who was at work—managing a hotel—more than she was at home. Grif lived off pizza delivery and made home horror movies with an old Super 8. He made the pale, yellow front of his suburban house terrifying. Otherwise, it only stood out for its lack of personal touches and a white-door garage that took up half of the house. In these movies, Grif overlay grainy images of kids wearing masks and sitting in rocking chairs, whispering lines lifted from his nan's creepy old poetry books. The background noise was all deep minor chords, singularly pounded and sustained on his nan's out-of-tune piano.

Grif, running his index finger across his straight-cut black bangs, invited Gerry in for a game of video soccer and some Cokes. The first driving pulse of the video game's soundtrack merged with the ringing in Gerry's head. Or maybe it was the sugar and caffeine in the consecutive Cokes he slammed. He got to trash talking, said no way no Goth art nerd could do him in footie. Grif's hands went up, fake shaking like he was so terrified.

"What are you if not an art nerd, Gerry?"

Gerry was Grif's creepiest actor, but his newer friends were actually darker, more entertaining.

The sun sneaked down. Grif got up mid-game and started filming Gerry scoring and raising the roof, singing, "Ring the alarm, I don't want to stay calm Yo, I'm about to rip this psalm, when the mic is gripped my lyrics do split up." Gerry cracked and pulled on another Coke and said the lights in Grif's house were crazy. The stranger part came when Grif's nan got home early, sat with Gerry on the couch and took over for Grif, playing video soccer. Grif's nan, despite her age, felt to Gerry like a young, super-fun aunt. He called her by her first name: Amor. He fantasized about her adopting him, though he was not sure Grif was the kind of brother he'd want. She tied up the game and took the lead lickety-split. She smiled at Gerry with her lipstick worn like the girls he saw in a magazine full of partial nudity he found in the woods, not far from the school, next to an abandoned fire pit. One time, Amor kissed him goodbye right on the lips and he still wondered if it counted as his first kiss. He remembered about his deal with Jennifer.

"What time is it?"

Gerry usually hated leaving Grif's—it meant going home—but he was motivated this day. He grabbed his schoolbag and paper bag and bolted into the early-evening darkness. There were no stars, no moon, just a glint from the headlights of Jennifer's dad's Civic. So much for that then. A relief, but a disappointment. He imagined telling her about boxing, wondered if it was better to talk about his victory over Khrys or play up his hard-fought loss to Shaughnessy, maybe go for sympathy. Either way, she would have plenty of questions so it wouldn't be hard to know what to say, he'd just follow her beautiful lead. Gerry fired the newspaper behind their screen door, waved to her dad and jogged downhill toward home, ears faintly ringing.

What happened there was nothing. Gerry's father said that was why he planted flowers every spring; their blossoming was one thing to look forward to. Gerry knew it was really atonement for not appreciating his mother when she had been there. But his father was right about the nothing—the nothing of 50 television channels, including the listings channel. Nothing was old movies and new video games and school and the weekday paper route. Nothing used to be Friday night Yahtzee games with best friends number one and two, Drew and Long. When they weren't around, nothing was damming the stream behind Grif's house with rocks and sticks and mud. Nothing was better then, before it involved trying not to feel things.

Sometimes pain could be oxygen, the feel of fresh air when you came up from the water after a long, deep dive in the pool. Back at Jason and Shaughnessy's house, Jason's precise jabs were a heart jolt. They staggered Gerry back, sucking in that leather smell, smiling, brain left on the stove too long. He flicked sweat from his hair. His biceps were weighted in fire.

It was like in Grade 6, when he and Grif dug up a knee-high bolder and lifted it together, veins outside their skin, and hauled it to the stream to dam it. Until he was 12, Gerry thought "dam it" and "damn it" were the same. That boulder was the best piece of dam they moved. The sticks and mud and garbage they surrounded it with were washed away by the next day. The boulder stayed.

Gerry jabbed at Jason. Shaughnessy, from the corner, "Yeah, yeah, stick and move. Seriously, you're doing it."

Jason knew exactly what was coming, slipped everything and countered.

Gerry blocked a few and sucked a few into the ribs. He held Jason by the arms to slow him down. Khrys made them break. Professional. They hugged it out and Jason told him he was improving.

When they split a beer in the kitchen, Gerry almost spilled about his deal with Jennifer. Who cared what she did, fuck it. But, impressed as they would have been, he kept it for himself, reached down and pet Shaughnessy and Jason's always-meowing cat. "Beer is making me hungry," he said.

Shaughnessy grabbed the cat and threw it in the microwave. He said his cousin told him cats were delicious. He was always picking on little things. Still, Gerry was shocked when he turned the microwave on and shouted, "Cat for lunch!" The cat was nearly 20 years old and half-blind. It sat there, rotating in the microwave, oblivious. It sniffed Gerry out every time he came over, leaving its white hairs all over his dark track pants. He loved that it had survived 15 years of Shaughnessy.

Gerry charged at Shaughnessy, shoved him out of the way and opened the microwave, pulled the cat out and stroked its head, whispering coochie-coos. The others gave a kind of joint, singular laugh. The cat yowled and bit Gerry, who yelped and dropped it. He snarled and yelled at his friends, asking them how they'd like it.

Shaughnessy said, "Cat don't like you, dude."

Gerry grabbed Shaughnessy's hoodie and tried to drag him to the open microwave to shove his head in. Shaughnessy shoved Gerry back, punched him in the side of the head, no glove. Gerry smelled iron, tasted metal. He stumbled like a slow realization, grabbing at his head, wondering if this second hard blow would stop the ringing, like in a cartoon. He muttered a fuck-you excuse and, fighting tears, grabbed his coat, backpack, and paper bag and stumbled onto the snowy deck. Blood spilling over his ear, no one left to cry to. Maybe Jennifer.

How his mother used to rant. Thermos full of cold, black coffee, up for a swig and down quick. "That pipsqueak is a mimic." Talking about some neighbour who hit the thrift store after she learned Gerry's mother went there every Friday night. The whole idea was that the store was empty. She bought day-old roses for Gerry's dad, who at the time had no interest in flowers. "Status-seeking phony" is what she called women she loathed, never bitch or witch or whore or anything biblical. She once said of Grif's nan, shouting over the vacuum she controlled with her thermos-free hand, "That woman's whole gluten-free diet is a sham. She doesn't need rid of gluten. The only impurity she suffers is the scum clogging her brain." Up-down the thermos. She sent Gerry to grab a flashlight so she could inspect for any missed dust.

Staring at the darkness of Jennifer's house, Gerry wished for a flashlight. To inspect for danger. Jennifer's lights were off and it was just past the darkest time of year. Gerry stared at the void where her house should have been, dreaming of flesh and thinking about his mother.

His mother departed at 44. She had a hard laugh that turned her face into a watershed of wrinkles. She used it sparingly, preferring to shout. Still, she always found him quickly in the dark. He woke often from nightmares of drowning. Her voice Betty Boop singing, "I Wanna Be Sedated" like a lullaby, his peace bubble, his refuge. He thought The Ramones were a children's group until Crystal played the original for them. Gerry's mother insisted on silence in the early morning and early evening hours. That's when she hit the phones to make her sales. Every day was an opportunity, she said, and every night a threat. They were already wealthy; she was a regional director at a bank. She told Gerry she'd hit the glass ceiling, so in her spare time she was climbing pyramids, selling telecommunications devices, insurance, financial services, health and beauty products, adult-only toys he later learned had to do with sex. There was a Tupperware party where every lady wore a skirt and lipstick and had her hair up. Their individual characters showed only in how bright the apron they chose from his mother's collection.

Staring at the void of Jennifer's house in the dark, he forced his mind off his mother. He thought about the house in front of him, how it appeared in daylight. It was textbook: five rectangles and two triangles, one over the garage and one over the larger of the two upstairs windows. Grey vinyl covered everything. Framed in white gutters that Jennifer's dad cleaned while the rest of the family was at church. Gerry approached the brown metal door, felt his knuckles on it, heard the ethereal creak as it opened.

He imagined his mother answering, her lipstick and apron a matching watermelon pink. Phone cradled between ear and shoulder, saying, "Who cares if it's a pyramid? If it makes you money and you get to be your own boss." Then whispering, "What do you want for supper, Gerald?"

A ring of light surrounded her then swallowed her, and into her place stepped Jennifer, eyes repellent wonder at his presence on her doorstep, skin pale-yellow and so plain compared to his mother. She frantically waved him away, like they had never made a deal. Her father was there now, stepping in front of her, reaching at his head, Gerry flinching. Jennifer's father's hands were soft but steady, so unlike his father's. He tilted Gerry's chin. "You're bleeding very badly," he said. "Come in and let's see if I can fix that up. We might need to get you to the hospital." Gerry tried to say yes but he was overcome with nausea and dizziness and tears as he stepped into the house. If he could just avoid Jennifer's eyes, he might be protected there.

OPERATION NIBLET

Zoëy teaches Gerry—who has always been in love with animals and every year paints several landscapes featuring majestic moose in wide-open fields—about how people think animals are property but they're not; they're sentient and have a right to live and enjoy smelling and tasting and seeing beauty. Eating them is wrong, and he won't do it anymore.

Terry and Sue, their other roommates, are also vegans. They are much more radical than Zoëy. They have each served time. Terry was convicted of assaulting a security guard and Sue snatched a wad of cash off an inattentive bank teller and burned it, setting off the fire sprinklers. Gerry loves their stories of defiance and lockup, like Bonnie and Clyde if they'd survived all those bullets from the posse. Zoëy is captivated by their ideas and questions them like a reporter seeking the perfect sound bite.

Maybe it is the weed, the fact that Gerry smokes and Terry and Sue don't, but when they all sit together on the front porch he is often stunned into silence by the things Terry and Sue say. Their words seem hazy and unfathomable but he loves listening anyway. He loves it when they call people pussies—he hadn't expected that from lesbians.

But he is also glad they aren't night owls like him and Zoëy. When Sue stands and holds her hands out to help Terry up, and leads her by the hand, inside to their shared room, it is the happiest moment of Gerry's daily routine. It is when he gets Zoëy alone and they can talk about her more nuanced ideas.

At such a time he tells Zoëy about his mother, specifically about his experience witnessing the moose the day she departed, how the majestic animal gave him strength to carry on despite the loss, how he had had many dreams of moose since, of being a half-moose half-man unsuccessfully harvesting wild rice with hooves, and of his previous life as a (possibly female) member of the Moose Clan of the Mamaceqtaw people of what is now called Wisconsin.

As he speaks he tries to read her eyes but as usual her Mona Lisa's visage reveals nothing of whatever she might be feeling. Inside she could be laughing or crying or wondering how she came to be alone with this maniac. When he finishes his story he fights, for the two hundredth time, the impulse to lean in and kiss her, and he wonders why he fights the impulse when his victory over it gives him only regret. Several minutes pass in the quiet of the city night. Gerry searches the sky and sees a blurred light that might be a bright star or a muted streetlight on a distant hill.

"It's a great metaphor for civilization," Zoëy finally says. "How it's taken ownership over everything and you could never accept that. Could you, Gerry? So, your very wildness prevents you from living in any kind of traditional way." She pulls out a baggie of weed from her jeans. "Speaking of which, do you know about the animal testing going on at Dal?"

He shakes his head.

"It's totally insane. They drill holes into the brains and eyes of kittens, puppies, rabbits, and mice while they're still alive, just to install things—poisons, monitors. When the experiment is done they kill them."

"Why would they do that?" Gerry said, horrified.

"Trying to cure blindness, stuff like that. They kill them by the millions in labs all over the world."

"Because they think they're our property," Gerry says.

"What would your Mamaceqtaw people think of that, Gerry?"

He shrugs and accepts the joint from her. "I think maybe the Moose Clan would think it's our job to fight back."

"That's what Terry said when I told her about it. That we have to fight back."

Gerry takes a toke. He tells Zoëy about the time he and Drew and Long tried to free a local drug dealer's pit-bull puppies, when he was nine years old. He expects her to laugh but there is no reason to. She is a serious person. He appreciates that about her because it makes him realize he's played the clown too many times in his life.

"I wish I'd known you then," she says.

He smiles, feeling like there may not come a better time to kiss her. But he is always uncertain of her meaning. Does she wish she'd known him then because they are soul mates? Maybe because he was so badass back then but he had gone soft. Maybe she wishes she'd known him then and taught him these things before he got so suburbanized.

"Maybe that's what we should do at the vivisection lab," she says, smiling in earnest, showing her slightly crooked teeth on the bottom, and the more perfect ones on top, overbiting slightly, as if embarrassed by what is happening underneath them. If he kissed her would that be a problem or would the fullness of her lips cushion the blow?

"The mother dog left me with a limp for weeks. I'm lucky I didn't get rabies."

"These are bunny rabbits and mice, Gerry," she says. "And a few puppies. No angry mamma dogs."

He knows he'll do it if she is serious. He'll do anything she asks. He wishes he could make them kids again so she could know him at that age, whatever her reasoning.

"How do we get in?" he says.

Terry and Sue prove invaluable in what they called

Operation Niblet, after the kind of wound Gerry might sustain should a bunny rabbit react as the drug dealer's dog did in his last animal heist. They come up with an elaborate plan to break into the lab and release as many mice and rabbits as they can into Point Pleasant Park, take a few kittens and puppies to give friends as pets. They spend several days scoping the place, walking around it from a comfortable distance then sneaking in with help from a sympathetic friend of a friend who does custodial shift work there. They get floor plans from the university archives and map out an escape route.

They borrow a friend's dark green minivan and take out the backseat to make room for the cages. Terry will drive. Sue and Zoëy will be lookouts. The janitor they know will help them get in without tripping alarms. Gerry gets the glory job. "You're skinny and strong and I bet you can run fast," Terry says. "The cages are only locked with padlocks, so you can bust them open with a hammer and chisel."

Gerry has a mild adrenaline rush thinking about it. He agreed to participate in a criminal mission for the sake of a hippie girl. A hippie girl he happens to love. He's gone insane. "Ever hear the expression 'herding cats'?" he says.

"You grab whatever you can carry, leave the rest running around the building, wreaking havoc. And smash the shit out of every computer you see, take any disks you find."

"What will that accomplish?"

"The PETA freaks haven't accomplished shit," Terry says. "All their sternly worded letters and listserv groups. Useless. They go right on torturing and killing. No animals are saved by that bullshit."

He doesn't see how this will be any different, which makes the risk he is taking all the more absurd. Zoëy. She is so hot she makes him physically ill, and apparently mentally ill too. It makes no sense, but he can't stop thinking it: if he can get through this thing unscathed, then he can kiss her.

The plan is simple: All Gerry has to do is go to a basement window at exactly 3:00 a.m., a window that is never used but will be unlocked by their inside person, who will have also popped in earlier in the evening to turn off the alarm. The building is patrolled by campus security, but Terry reassures him it is vacant from 3:00 to 4:00. Gerry will go alone, dressed all in black with a balaclava because of the video surveillance, with the hammer and chisel hanging from his belt. The green minivan will be outside waiting the whole time.

He is two minutes late arriving, but that leaves plenty of time. He glances around for the van but doesn't see it. It will be there. He pulls the window open and crawls down, ducks under the ceiling pipes, and runs to the stairs on the far side of the room.

The stairs are sunk in darkness but he's been told there are eight large steps. As he counts seven there is a thunderous crash. He feels blood rush to his nose, making him dizzy. He turns on his flashlight to look at a heavy metallic door. It has blood on it. His blood. They gave him the wrong number of stairs. He's been lured into this insanity by amateurs, gifted bullshitters clueless when it comes to capers.

"Fuck," he whispers. Before his blood can dry, he wipes it off with the inside of one of his black gloves. The inside is white cotton. He spits and wipes, spits and wipes, wondering about DNA, and realizes he is damned either way. The best he can do is clear up the visual evidence. He looks at his watch: 3:07. "Fuck."

He tries the door. Locked. "Fuck. For fuck's sake!"

He kicks it and hurts his foot. There is no way in. He flashes his light down the stairs and descends, willing his muscles to experience each movement, ignoring his heart pounding at the back of his eyeballs. It takes him several minutes to get back to the window, and he feels a surge of relief when it opens. He has tried his best and there is nothing left to do, though his chest heaves for the failure to earn that kiss that has been staring him in the face each night, so clear from such distance.

Gerry pulls himself onto the grass and looks again for the van. No sign of it. No matter. With no animals he can ditch the balaclava and bloodied gloves and walk home.

"Hold up a minute," a voice says.

Gerry glances over his left shoulder and freezes at the sight of a security guard ambling toward him, who on seeing Gerry in his all-black balaclava suit freezes to his spot. Gerry wishes he could stroll to the guard and put his arm around him and point to the trees at some hidden camera. Ha ha, what a farce!

Instead, Gerry bolts, slips on the wet grass, and lurches forward into a puddle. He gets up and runs again, his feet squishing with each step. Gerry sprints south and cuts to a side street all the way to Point Pleasant Park. He scans his surroundings for the van. He is afraid to look back. He is pretty sure he's lost his security friend. He collapses under a tree, lowers his head, pinches his nose and laughs until tears cool his cheeks. Someday he will give the boys back home a huge laugh with this story. For now, he wants to see Zoëy.

In the backseat of the van Zoëy apologizes a million times for not showing up. She explains how they got diverted. A cop pulled them over on their way, she says. They were so nervous about the slim possibility of that very occurrence they were driving too far below the speed limit. The cop, on seeing what looked like three dykes crawling along at 2:30 a.m., was suspicious. But they were dressed normally—for them—Terry and Sue with their multicoloured hair, khaki pants, and button-up shirts, and Zoëy with her dreads and hoodie and tight brown cords. The cop looked in the back of the van and found a couple dozen small animal cages.

Terry told the cop she was a vet, to which he said, "Get out of the vehicle." Zoëy's voice goes low to imitate the cop. "All of you." He checked their pockets and ran their licenses. Found nothing. They weren't wanted for anything anymore and there was no evidence of any wrongdoing. He followed them around after they drove away, stayed with them at every turn. Finally they went home and hung out quietly until the cop car drove off. By the time they got to the park, Gerry was huddled up shivering by the trunk of a Norway maple.

"I was afraid to walk home dressed like a thief," Gerry says. His adrenalin-induced arrhythmia fails to keep him warm and he shivers. She puts an arm around him and the other hand on his chest. He had been half-asleep when he heard the minivan passing by, had to jump from that state and pound on the back of it before they left him.

"Gerry?" Zoëy had whispered when they opened the rear sliding door and he climbed in. "Did you get any animals?"

Gerry had burst out laughing. He couldn't help it. He was soaked and covered in mud and blood and hadn't come within a hundred metres of a live animal except the dogs on Tower Road howling at picture windows.

He looks at Zoëy's serious face, concerned though even as she comforts him he can't be sure if it is for him or the animals. He tries to mirror her stoicism on his own face. He has been afraid since finding the door locked in the lab basement that the futility of this effort will not only erase her respect for him, but his for her. He needn't have worried. The approach was all wrong, trying to attack systematic cruelty with a hammer and chisel and balaclava and minivan. But her intentions are pure. Operation Niblet had failed but she will change the world and he will be right there with her.

"The door was locked," he says. "Couldn't get in at all."

Before she can answer he leans forward and kisses her. When she kisses back, as if trying to douse a flame with her spit, his heart slows for the first time since climbing into the lab's basement.

In the weeks following the failure of Operation Niblet, Terry, Sue, and Zoëy try to convince him to have another go at the lab, and that their inside person can take care of that unexpected locked door, and usually security is nowhere near the lab between 3:00 and 4:00 and it must have been a busy night on campus or something.

He doesn't regret his actions. They gave him the courage or the rush he needed to kiss Zoëy. But busting animals loose from the joint isn't his style. He is more a thinker, and an artist. The failed caper and subsequent fumbling through Zoëy's loose clothing to her skin inspires several new paintings, all pounded into canvas while Zoëy sleeps after their intense fucking, during which their hands grope at every curve and seam in an attempt to become one multi-orgasmic body. Gerry can't sleep afterward; he is jolted awake by the intensity of her legs wrapped around him and he shakes as he paints with the urgency of night, the need to finish before dawn.

The paintings aren't obvious interpretations of animal rights or love or the clear association between the two in Gerry's mind. They are pictures of dew on spider webs and piglets running through dandelions, waves exploding on rocks, and other snippets of glory etched in his memory by orgasm. Such pictures have no more hope of changing the world than smoking a joint and shooting the shit on the porch, he realizes, but they come more naturally to him. And he fears going to jail, alone, having to find another new identity in order to fit in with another new group. He'd rather stay here with Zoëy.

The paintings are his only answer to Zoëy's escalating demands for radical action of some sort. He nods and kisses her and goes down on her until she forgets about non-human animals and he paints the rest of the night.

The more they fuck the more radicalized she

becomes—the more obsessed with proving to him that a revolution could work—and the more she rants on revolution the more obsessed he becomes with fucking her. She gives him books about the world's great revolutions and he buys her a copy of the *Kama Sutra*. When she asks him to consider what would be lost if they do nothing, he takes it as a threat to stop fucking him.

"All right," he tells her, "tell me about your revolution then." He hopes she has something better than a bigger and crazier version of Niblet. As she spoons him, he feels safe and protected—as he once felt with his high school buddies—and he knows that happiness is something so elusive a man will do anything to keep it once he's found it. He laughs aloud. A bigger and crazier version of Operation Niblet is exactly what he is going to get.

WITHOUT MOTHERHOOD

When Gerry was 11, his mother died laughing. She had a big laugh, but used it sparingly. On a visit to a friend's place she got giggling, watching some comic on television. Her body seized up and died. Gerry wondered if it was a reaction to laughter, if she'd been allergic. Maybe that was why she had been so serious. The friend called Gerry's father from emerge, where his mother had just been pronounced. Gerry's father yelled at Gerry.

The day after she died, Gerry lay in his bed listening very hard for her knock. Harder. Whether it was there or not, he had to hear that knock. His mother had been a pain, in control of everything around her. Her death made no sense. How could she be gone? How could she not be in control? He needed to hear her again. Gerry closed his eyes, focusing hard. Harder. Until he saw her outside his door, faint, faded, but there, just there. Gerry squeezed his eyes harder shut, bringing her into focus. He could see her left hand, making a loose fist, rising over his alabaster bedroom door.

Knock.

Knock knock.

Had he heard it? He thought he had. His eyes were

open; he was looking at the door, following the lines of its rectangles.

"Hello?"

No response, just emptiness.

His mother was gone.

To make any sense of her departure would take greater concentration. He closed his eyes. Squeezed. Until he saw the loose fist, her skin smooth except for that arrow-shaped vein pulsing over her index knuckle with her swift movements. Rising to strike.

Knock knock knock.

Gerry?

Yes, there she was, calling his name, more gently than she had before…

Gerald?

More forceful now.

Gerald? We need to talk. Open up.

"Um!" Um? She would think it a wasted syllable. He had conjured her, so why should he be intimidated?

Gerald?

Soft again. Fading. He squeezed his eyes tighter. "Yes, Mother." If he opened his eyes, would she be dead again?

Can you open?

Why had she come back? Something to say? Yes. That's why dead people came back. They could come back if there was an unresolved issue. Must have been something really bad. His father. Something about his father, the lump. She was going to prepare him for life with a useless parent.

Gerald!

"Coming!"

His mother was the bread winner, the source of their wealth. She was a materialist. He wished she shared his taste in possessions. They lived by the lake. He told his friends the house was 10,000 square feet. Three floors plus finished basement for a family of three, original artwork on the walls, wood stove, decorative fireplace, glass ornaments and pretty things, a black Jag and electric-blue Jeep. At school he was a rich kid, but he cared less than anyone about his brand-name clothes. Mother was appalled at how Gerry got himself filthy, building dams in the stream behind his friend Grif's house. Didn't bother to tuck the polo into the Dockers. Gerry would have preferred jogging pants and a hoodie. He wanted a Nintendo Entertainment System, a pool table and a basketball hoop.

"Too ghetto," Mother had said.

Gerry rose from his bed, eyes still closed, stood feeling the soft fabric of his pajamas hanging over him. In his mind's eye, he could see the alabaster door, but if he opened his eyes she might go away. He tried to remember the state of his bedroom floor. Was it covered in Lego and GI Joes? He imagined himself happy toeing around books and clothes and sporting equipment, bowing with a flourish and snatching open the door. Why couldn't she open the door herself? Maybe she couldn't, physically.

"Entrez!" he said. He sat on his bed and there she was, sitting next to him, not faded. Fully present. She had only needed permission. She pulled a face at the sight of him in his pajamas. It was almost noon. The dirty things strewn across the floor.

"We need to talk, Gerald." His dead mother, sitting on the corner of his bed, wanting to talk. "I always liked that picture." She pointed at a self-portrait by a New York artist friend of hers, a curly-haired old guy with octagon-shaped glasses and four chins. She had him ship it up for Gerry's birthday. She stared at it a minute before Gerry realized she had a lonely tear pushing its way through her mascara.

"Jesus what's wrong?"

Her body had always been in motion, rearranging furniture or art, tidying papers while talking on the phone. Always smooth, never hurried.

"Please don't swear, Gerald. Please, please don't swear. You're too intelligent to take after your father."

"I don't take after him."

"There's something I have to tell you. You know I cannot stay."

Gerry nodded. He was going to be stuck with his father.

"I won't be all that far away. We'll find each other again."

Gerry nodded, not understanding.

"I'm going to Jersey."

Gerry squeezed his eyes tighter, struggling to keep

them closed. Jersey? "What the hell?"

"Don't swear, Gerald."

"Jersey?"

"It's minimum security."

Gerry exhaled through the nose, not laughing at all. "*New* Jersey?" Gerry wanted his useless father. His father in his mother's place was oblivion.

"Do you remember I worked at the bank, back in New York?"

Before Father went off the deep end into fits of muttering rage. Some huge bank headquartered in New York. Gerry was at the alternative school with kids as weird as him. Father used to get off work by 5:00 to get Gerry from after-school programs. In the mornings, he dropped Gerry at school.

"There was an ... opportunity. To borrow. Well, you know what embezzle means?"

Gerry knew it from *Weekend at Bernie's*. Mother said she took advantage of some smudged numbers, entering them into a new computer system herself. "I suppose I was thinking about your father. If we had more money he could do the things he talked about: the inventions, his own business. I thought about that tiny little apartment, you remember how crowded that was?"

Gerry nodded. In his memory he could play with his toys in the stairwell, watching his slinky work its magic, his plastic Cowboys working for higher position on his plastic Indians.

"Your father and I were always tripping over each other. It was just a little bit less in the computer, and a little bit of cash in my pocket. Not much that first time."

His perfect mother had been a thief all along.

"It's easier to do wrong than right."

Gerry would agree to anything.

"This language you're using. It's an easy way to express your anger. Try harder to find the right words." She hugged him and he clung to her, eyes shut tight, tried to find the smell of her, the Yves Saint Laurent, feel the coolness of her fingers. She was never a person who hugged. "I know you're a good boy, Gerald, but you have to be better."

He took another breath of her. "Okay."

"By the time we moved here…"

"We were rich." She had taken more and more, until the accountants got suspicious and they had to go on the lam in Canada. She took that job here, at a smaller bank, and she did her multi-level sales things. It took them a while to catch her. Gerry's mother was a badass fugitive, Bonnie to Clyde, only her Clyde had no clue.

"I must depart." She kissed the bridge of his nose, her lips chemical wet.

"No, Mother."

"Be strong. Your father's not well."

"You can't."

"Our time is up. Your father thinks we came here

for a change. Our little secret okay?"

She gave a last slow wave and ... what? She didn't disappear exactly, or walk through a wall or the closed alabaster door either. Gerry's eyes had stayed closed. She stood a moment before the door, as if contemplating the prospect of walking through it. He opened his eyes. She wasn't there. Of course not. She was departed.

"Father." Gerry attempted to shout but it was a whisper. He tried to pound on the shed door but he tapped it. Nobody knew what the punishment was for entering Earl's shed while he was inventing. Gerry knocked again, a little louder. "Father?" No answer, just the beat of a hammer on something metallic. "Fuck it." He remembered, too late, his mother admonishing him not to swear.

He went for a walk. Uphill from the house was the new junior high, where Gerry would start Grade 7 in a week. He went the other way, toward the trailer park, down one long hill of rural highway and up another. The sidewalks were empty, which suited Gerry fine. The sun was setting with its usual late-summer dazzle. Gerry thought of his mother's otherwise perfect mascara, parted by a tear. Could it happen like that?

He sang a John Lennon song from before he was

born. "My Mummy's Dead." His friend Drew had shared with Gerry his great love of John Lennon. He switched tunes. "Mother, you had me, but I never had you." How articulate did Mother expect him to be? "Fuck her!" Gerry punched an old wooden mailbox with visions of his fist disintegrating it. It was more solid than it looked. He resolved to swear more. "Fucking cocksucking piece of cunt. Fucking so-called mailbox." He shook his hand, glaring at the mailbox.

"Don't fret, Ger."

He turned and there was Drew, butter-eyed and leaning forward against his bike.

"That mailbox had it coming."

Gerry half smiled, all the encouragement Drew needed to go into a bit about how every time he passed this mailbox it always had some smarmy remark. It insulted Drew's walk, his waddle, his weight and his mother. It had made crude sexual remarks about her. Drew leaned his bike against a tree and guided Gerry away from the mailbox and toward the trailer park. His arm was hot and sweaty and felt like it was holding him together.

"I'm really sorry for your loss, Ger."

"What loss?"

"Uh ... Ma told me. About..."

"Mother's going to prison, Drew."

Drew shook his head, looking almost panicked. He was rock steady but he didn't know how to handle Gerry's mother being a criminal. They walked in silence to the trailer park. They went to where the pavement ended and entered the dense woods. There were campsites covered with empty beer bottles, dead fire pits and cigarette butts. Gerry pushed past those and headed deeper into nowhere, until one tree blended into the next.

Drew spoke the obvious first. "I think we're lost." He was good in the woods; his family had taken Gerry on a couple of camping trips and they let him light the Coleman and showed him how to use a compass. If he thought they were lost, they were lost. Still Gerry pushed on, toward the last of the daylight, into a big open space about the size of a football field. They walked to the far side and sat on what would be the sidelines if the Lions and Bills were squaring off. Gerry put his head between his knees. He was drifting off when they heard a light rustling of branches. Gerry lifted his head and whispered Drew's name, clutched at his elbow. They scanned the horizon and saw, about 150 feet off to their right, a moose. It walked toward their general direction.

Drew gave a low, soft whistle. "Unbelievable." He put a hand on his knee and a finger to his lips. He spoke in a whisper. "An improbable fluke." Something his father might say.

For what felt like hours, but was probably ten or fifteen minutes, they watched the awkward giant walk across the field. Somehow she made no sound other than the occasional crack of a branch under her hooves, the sound of which made her stop, statue still, listening for potential danger, before resuming her funny moose walk—one leg at a time, first the rear left leg, then the front left, then the rear right, then the front right. On one long pause, Gerry saw that she rolled her pupils around. They filled most of her eye sockets under long lashes fancy women would kill for, with just a ridge of white showing around them. She took in the whole of the field. But because Gerry and Drew didn't move a muscle, she probably didn't register them against the edge of the clearing. She sniffed but there was no breeze. She swivelled her big furry ears. Gerry held his breath. Her bottom teeth jutted out, looking oddly human and pristine, like she'd just come from the dentist. It looked as if she were pondering something, the meaning of life or whether she would soon find a mate and become a mother, something greater than herself, taking on sole responsibility for a life other than her own. Without motherhood, what was a moose's purpose? Would a young moose's mother just up and die laughing, leaving her child alone? Maybe this moose was feeling like she had forgotten something, and wondered if she should go back and look for it.

Eventually she strode forward again, the flap of loose skin under her chin swaying side to side with each step. She was already fat, preparing for the winter ahead, impossibly heavy for her spindly legs.

When she reached the edge of the clearing, she

dropped to her front knees. Gerry thought for a moment some hunter had taken her down, and almost cried out because he could practically see the bullet tear through flesh, ripping through the upper part of the foreleg and into her lungs, gone before she could birth, nurture, raise her offspring to maturity. But there had been no shot. The moose had dropped to her knees of her own volition. She leaned her great head forward, munched at a patch of wildflowers. It would forever seem impossible, as though they could hear the munching sounds as the moose savoured her treat, like Gerry and Drew were sharing the snack with her. She picked the flowers clean and leaned back, rocked herself to her feet again.

Gerry and Drew sat, watching with hearts thundering, afraid and awed, sweating in the day's remaining heat. When the moose was gone, having crashed her way into a thicket, they sat as still as if she remained, not looking at one another or talking. Gerry thought about his mother, and wondered how Drew had heard about her criminal act.

Drew sat, not looking at Gerry. "I think I have a good idea of the right direction," he said. "We can push our way through the bramble, like a moose. Even if we can't find a path, we'll hit the trailer park or the main road." When he stood and walked toward the middle of the field, where the moose had been, Gerry followed. They squatted at a hoof print in a bit of muck, side by side. "Moose is an Algonquin word," Drew said.

"What does it mean?"

"Moose."

Drew pointed to a spot at the other side of the field where the trees looked less dense. He put his arm around Gerry. They walked out with no words, finding their way back to the trailer park and the sidewalk toward home.

"Twig eater," Drew said when they reached Gerry's house.

"What?"

"Moose means twig eater."

The stars were bright and Gerry's father was still in the shed, hammering, without much rhythm. Gerry went inside, made himself a peanut butter sandwich, and waited. His father couldn't stay out there forever. In the morning he had cereal and went back to the shed. Gerry pounded on the shed door, hard. The hammering stopped a moment, then resumed. He pounded again.

"What?"

"It's me. Gerry. Mother left."

The hammering resumed.

"Father!" Gerry unlatched and opened the door, stepped into the musky darkness, eyes squinted, seeing only sparks. "They took her." His voice was strained, throat constricted.

"What?" Father's silhouette emerged and, from that, a plaid wool shirt.

"She departed." He rushed forward, tripped over something heavy on the floor and wrapped his arms around Father's legs as he fell, snotting all over his thighs, feeling a rough hand on his cheek, and something small and hard: a little white pill.

"Take this, Kid. You'll be fine."

Gerry slipped the pill into his pocket. "What will we do without Mother?"

Earl turned back to his metal worktable and resumed pounding the bare table, harder, faster, with more emphasis. Gerry stepped out and looked at the stars reflected on the lake. He tossed the little white pill into the water and belched a single mighty curse word at the darkness. He languished over that word, stretched its syllable to its fullest possible length, so that any proximate ghosts or moose could hear it.

EL CAMINO

GERRY THOUGHT HE SHOULD drive since it was his idea to take the car. What an idiot.

Juan Jaime, who as a counterpoint to his short stature nicknamed himself Long when he first came to Canada, reminded Gerry and Drew that he was the only one who knew how to drive. His recently deceased father, the owner of the El Camino, used to take him to the Save-Easy parking lot on Sundays to teach him the gas, the brakes, and especially the clutch. There was once a group of high school kids there. They laughed as the car jerked and stalled, started and screeched as Long peeled an accidental strip.

"First gear first!"

"Ignore them," his dad had said. "You'll be driving a four-fifty-four smooth before they learn where the key goes."

Gerry rode shotgun and Drew jammed himself into the little space behind the seats. "Glad we gave the skinny guy all the room," Drew said.

"I have longer legs." Gerry bounced his knees for emphasis.

Long eased the El Camino out of the driveway and down the trailer park's main road. He pulled a sharp right into his neighbour's driveway.

"That's it?"

"No, Gerry, there's more."

Long put the stick in reverse and tried to get a good view over Drew. He didn't say so, but he needed Kang-Dae, the self-appointed king of the trailer park, to see him in the El Camino, lounging in style with his subdivision friends. He would kill Kang-Dae if he had the means, but of course he didn't. Maybe he could run him over with the El Camino. That would be good poetic justice, Kang-Dae's guts on his dad's tires, an exquisite end to the little pyramid scheme, Kang-Dae's local empire of dealers and bullies, who he called his bullet catchers. Kang-Dae's father had been a military policeman who fled South Korea as soon as the border clashes began, back in the 50s, and cheered the Yanks on from Canada. Kang-Dae once told Long that his dad carried the bitterness of their loss into his grave. He often took it out on rebellious Kang-Dae, who wasn't yet born when all that stuff started. Despite hating his father, Kang-Dae proudly wore green US Army t-shirts tailored for fitter men. They showed off his abnormally large biceps and stomach, rock hard and hungry.

Imagine killing a man like that. It would have put Long out of business, for one thing. He indulged himself a moment, thought about how killing Kang-Dae might go. If he could be patient. Wait for his growth spurt. It had to come eventually, didn't it? But even then, all Kang-Dae's top guys, Kevin and Mo and

Hong, they all owned handguns. They made a point of telling everyone about the action on them, the kick they gave when they practiced at the range. He couldn't imagine a single scenario that didn't end with his brains splattered somewhere. And it wouldn't bring his father back.

He eased the El Camino down the unpaved part of the road, first gear, 15 in a 20, past Kang-Dae's place. The big man was there, shovelling his driveway, wearing light blue jogging pants and a puffy black parka, open over his US Army shirt, with a big tomato stain in the middle of the chest. The snow was just starting up again.

Long's dad had figured they could make a better life in Canada. He and his wife could make more money and send lots of it back to his sisters—Long's aunties—so they could all get married properly. But it took all their money to immigrate and survive until they found work. Starting up a new business in Canada was too expensive, so they worked to pay rent and bills and buy food. The kind of jobs people would hire them for didn't pay much.

Every extra cent went back to the island, but the family wanted more. They didn't believe Long's dad when he told them how much rent was. The family said they must live in a mansion. Long's mother mailed Polaroids of their trailer. The Aunties called. They brought Grandma to the phone. They all stood around it yelling. "Liar! Liar! No way could that little box cost five hundred a month." It was lucky they couldn't spend much time yelling. Long distance cost a lot of money.

Long was also lucky Kang-Dae took an interest in him when he first moved in, put him to work selling pills to junior high kids and called him his "baby soldier." Kang-Dae had taught him first thing, "Everything is a pyramid, Brother. But this is the only one that really pays—cash only. And there's no paperwork, no inventory. It's all just networking, building your network and providing a service."

By Grade 9, everyone at school and in the trailer park knew Long. He was part of every fundraiser and went door to door collecting empties or selling chocolates, cheese, homemade Christmas decorations or whatever, and providing a little bit of weed, speed and acid for those who knew him best. He won all kinds of awards from his school for raising the most money, for sports teams, dances, science fairs and chess tournaments. It was all a hustle, requiring that he have more friends than anyone else. All it took was smiling, joking and talking talking talking. Long befriended everyone, including the kids everyone made fun of for being stupid skids. He was the only kid who was friends with caucasians, Blacks, Koreans, and Pakistanis. He asked people how they were doing, learned their names and the pronunciation, let them know he was there to make their lives easier, help them forget their pain. Unlike other people working for Kang-Dae, Long was never afraid to spread a little cash around, give a discount to his most loyal customers. They needed to know he could help, like a friend. He never dressed too flashy—he wore clean Nikes and polo shirts that fit well, but nothing over the top. He couldn't afford to anyways because all his earnings went back to the island. Kang-Dae sent the money through Western Union, with Long's love.

It never occurred to Long that his relatives would hate his dad more because of that money. To them, Long's generosity was proof they were doing better than his dad would admit. They sent a Christmas card addressed to Long, as if he were the man of the house. The look his dad gave him, his pride not letting him ask what was going on, that stretched, almost horrified expression on his face—it felt as if he'd called his own father a failure. When Long's grandmother died, it was him they called for funeral money. His grandmother had been the female head of the whole family, on the Pacific and the Atlantic. They had to send her to heaven the right way. They asked for an amount. Long gulped.

"Auntie," he said. "I will send it soon. I won't let you down."

It took a week.

When it came time to settle the till with Kang-Dae, Long took slow baby steps up the driveway and thought his story through. The door flew open the moment he knocked; Kang-Dae answered in a volatile mood.

"Get inside!"

Long stumbled into the kitchen, which was the main entryway for all the trailers, and shoved cash into Kang-Dae's hands.

Kang-Dae held it without looking at it. "Long, you are the only bullet catcher I can trust, kid. I'm serious. What if I told you I had to fuck up one of my most experienced colonels just yesterday for acting all fugazi? I will not tolerate insubordination. That's how wars are lost, son."

Long's knee buckled as Kang-Dae turned from him and spread the money over his kitchen table. He thought about running. It would only make things worse.

"That all?" Kang-Dae turned back.

Long launched into his prepared spiel. "Those frigging kids under me dropped a bag of pills cutting up through the swamp. I told them not to take shortcuts."

"I gave you a very clear, very fucking direct order. I told you to stick with trailer-park grunts."

The subdivision kids gave the operation more reach and money for less work, but it was pointless telling Kang-Dae that again. That wasn't how his pyramid worked. He wanted his bullet catchers to keep recruiting within a tiny radius. But there were only so many layers they could have under them before the levels got too thin. It was already happening. Kang-Dae didn't care. He just wanted to be the general. Long had never seen that so clearly before. *I will not tolerate insubordination.* He'd been foolish to think more money was the goal. That's why he'd gone broader. That's why he moved more product to farther away places. Kang-Dae had this weird notion of power, being the ultimate authority. He lived in a trailer and drove a hatchback.

"Sorry," Long said, head bowed. "I fucked up."

Kang-Dae turned away from the table and stepped toward Long, his big gut bumping his chest. He pushed Long backward, into the fridge. He punched the mini-freezer, leaving a lightened brown oval in the veneer. Kang-Dae breathed hot on Long's forehead. "You think you can fuck around with my network?"

Long felt a trickle of pee at the front of his underwear. He wasn't sure what was holding him up. It might have been Kang-Dae's belly, pressed against him. He wished he could collapse, but he didn't think he could move. He knew he should speak, let Kang-Dae know it was a mistake, that he would work for free to pay him back, that he would do whatever was required to make it right, to prove his loyalty. He whimpered.

Kang-Dae pressed into him harder, lowering his forehead into Long's, forcing eye contact. He smelled of canned tuna. "Listen Long. You've been a good soldier, right. But you are dispensable, okay. You crossed a line. That comes with a steeper price than you maybe realized."

Long managed, with effort, a slight nod, pushing their skulls against one another.

"Any of them subdivision brats you hired want to keep working send them to me. Directly. Get the fuck out."

When squad-car lights flashed in Long's window, he instinctively ran to his room and hid under the covers with his cat. His little brother Mateo followed and climbed in. Then it was Leonarda, his mother. His sister Angel followed, heaving sobs, but she spoke softly so he could barely hear. "Daddy was shot. He's dead."

That was obviously wrong. Long's dad had kissed Long when he went out that evening. He had specifically said that he would see Long again when he got back. He said he would not be late. There were important things he did not mention. Like never coming back. Like dying. Like Long having to live the rest of his life without him.

Long's father was universally loved. Even the sisters who wanted all his money affectionately called him their little bandit. When Long opened his mouth to request clarification from his mother, a howling animal sound emerged. The cat thrust its face into his, its purr urging him to settle, accept the ferocity of its devotion. Long, his siblings and his mother huddled together, crying and wailing, as the cat tried to squeeze its way between them.

"He's dead," his mother said, her voice gentle with words cruel and evil.

She had to go to the morgue to identify the body. She said the cops did not know who did it. They wanted to talk to all of them.

"I want to come with you," Long said. He could prove everybody wrong and see with his own eyes that someone other than his father had been killed, that there had been a misidentification by the police.

"Stay with Mateo," his mum said.

It wouldn't have happened like that on the island. They would have all gone together. But the Canadian cops said it wasn't good for the kids to see their father with bullets in his guts and head and chest. On the island they would have called in the whole family and hunted the killers themselves.

"They said he was buying drugs," Angel said after their mum was gone. "They wanted to search the trailer but Mummy wouldn't let them. They said they would come back with a warrant."

Mateo cried and Long held him close.

"Daddy doesn't do drugs," Long said.

"I know." His sister knew everything. "Why do you think they would say he was buying drugs?"

Long couldn't look at her. He remembered how their dad drank Keith's beer every weekend. Once in a while, he'd get drunk, start slapping their mum on the butt and tell dirty jokes. Their mum would give him a little shove and say go sleep it off. He would grab her hand and pull her down the hall, the two of them giggling. On weeknights, Long's dad didn't drink at all. He couldn't have a single beer without feeling sick in the morning and his shift started at 5:00 a.m. Long's mum had to get up with him at 4:00 so he could drop her by the recycling depot, where her shift started at 6:00. He picked her up again on the way home. There was no time for getting high. He had gone to Spryfield to meet a buddy for a beer. The buddy worked at the Prince George Hotel. He was trying to get their dad a job there, but their dad never showed. They found his body in a parking lot outside a known dealer's apartment.

Long didn't know if Mateo understood any of it, but his body began to convulse after Long thought he'd fallen asleep against his chest. His sister scowled. Long put his free arm around her, and she put one around him. He could feel the muscles in her shoulder. She smelled of perfume an admirer had bought her. He nestled into her neck and cried. She squeezed him and pulled him closer, extracting a sliver of pain. In a few minutes, his brother stopped convulsing and fell asleep for real. Their mother came home and climbed into bed with them so they could have someone full grown and full strength to hold. They fell asleep across the three single beds the kids had pushed together. The cat slept on Long's chest.

They slept a few hours before the cops arrived in four different cars with lights flashing. This time they had a warrant. The family stood outside in the snow while the cops tore through everything they owned and left it on the floor. Long was without drugs. Kang-Dae had a pit tunnelled under his neighbour's trailer for them. They were covered with firewood and large tarps. When the cops finished with the trailer, they searched his dad's 1970 turquoise El Camino. It was his one Canadian-life luxury, and one more reason his sisters thought he was holding out on them. It cost him $1,500.

Each cop took one of them in the backseat of a cruiser and asked questions. "What did your father do for a living? Did he know any drug dealers at work? Did he ever sell drugs? Were any of his friends drug dealers? Did he go out a lot at night? Did he ever touch you? You know? In bad places? In bad ways?" It kept going.

They talked to Long's mum the longest. "They offered us counselling," she said.

"No," Long said.

"No shrinks," Angel said.

"We don't need to talk to anybody about it except our family."

Long's mother sent him for pizza and cigarettes. He held out his hand.

"You have plenty of money. Why would you need mine?"

By the time Long returned to school, everyone knew. Everybody stared and nobody said anything except, "Hi." Some of the girls took the chance to give him hugs. Drew and Gerry didn't say much either, thankfully. Drew put his arm on Long's shoulder without any of his usual smart-assery. Long rested his head on Drew's hand and was relieved no one called him gay.

Long put his tears away, as his mother used to say when he was small. It was good to know his friends were there. But he had no idea what they could do. Jesus himself would not be bringing back his father. Why did he feel like he had to reassure them? "I'll be okay."

Gerry gave him an awkward pat on the head.

Long went for a walk at lunch, thinking he might keep walking all the way home. He was still at the edge of the schoolyard when he heard his father's name.

"Maybe you could paint a portrait of him. Don't you think?"

Drew was talking to Gerry. Those two could be

brothers.

"Yeah, maybe. He's a tough little shit don't you think? But Jee-sus fuck, his dad gets murdered in a drug deal. And Long's a dealer? Jee-sus."

Long shouted to them. "It was not a drug deal!"

Others could think that. These two should have known better. Even they didn't know Long was responsible. They spun around wearing painted grins.

"Hey, brother."

"Hey."

"Gerry was just saying he's going to paint a picture of your dad. Like a portrait. For your family."

Gerry giggled.

"That drug-deal story is bullshit. You know my father never touched drugs."

"Okay, yeah man. I just can't believe he's gone."

Drew surprised Long, put both arms around him. Gerry patted him on the back.

Long pulled away, wanting anything but sympathy. "I was going for a walk. You two can come. If you want."

They walked toward a logging trail that cut to the main road. "One thing I don't get," Drew said after several minutes of footsteps on gravel. "What was your dad doing in Spryfield?"

"My dad *works* in Spryfield," Gerry said. "You think it's Beirut or something?"

"My dad says he wouldn't go near there without his Winchester."

"*My* dad goes there every day."

"*Your* dad *is* on drugs."

"True. It's true. So, what's happening with your dad's El Camino?"

Long hated that car. It wasn't even worth anything.

"Sitting in the driveway. Why?"

"Maybe we should take it out. Give it a last ride?"

Long bit his tongue before he could call Gerry an idiot. "Okay. Yeah, let's do it."

They looked confused.

"Daddy's funeral was tiny you know. Grandma's funeral? Six hundred people. I paid for it."

They nodded without a clue what he meant. Paying for one funeral had caused the other. He had been massively, unforgivably, stupid to rip off the king of the trailer park. There was no going back.

"Let's go."

He ran ahead of them, down a long white slope to the woods, the balls of his feet peppering the recent snow, the rest of him flying over it.

Drew gave a mock squeal and chased. Gerry followed. "Wait, wait. Are you sure, Long?"

"One day this four-fifty-four engine will be yours." Long's dad had said that a few times, revving the horses in neutral, patting the dashboard.

He had polished it inside out, every weekend.

From behind the wheel of his father's El Camino, Long saw Kang-Dae glance over and bend double, laughing. He gave them two thumbs way up from his bent-over position, fully exposing the stain on his army t-shirt. Psycho.

From the passenger seat, Gerry returned the thumbs up with a big goofy grin.

"Kang-Dae had my father killed," Long said.

"What? No he didn't."

"He did."

He had no particular desire to prove it; saying it aloud one time was enough. Drew and Gerry didn't say anything until Long turned onto the rural highway toward town.

"Over drugs?"

It was a world they knew nothing about because they didn't need to. No one asked them for money. Not for a wedding or a funeral or to buy goddamn pizza.

"Insubordination."

"Say the word," Drew said. "I'll get every single one of my cousins down to the trailer park and they'll tear his place to pieces and beat the shit out of him."

Not meaning to, Long laughed. He leaned forward and laughed so hard he hit his head on the steering wheel, honking the horn.

"My cousins are hardcore, man. One of them is a stevedore. Know what that means? Teamster connections. Those guys are animals. They stick together. If I tell them you're family, they'll do anything."

Long was genuinely touched, and fascinated that anyone could have understand so little. As if a bunch of cousins in a union could be more fearsome than someone who would kill for obedience.

"Thanks, Drew. Really."

Drew didn't know of Kang-Dae's obsession with staying atop his pyramid, or how hard it was to keep a bunch of dope-selling kids in line. Nor did he know of the man's temper, his earned reputation for violence, how many times that fist connected with flesh instead of fridge. All his daddy issues parlayed into wannabe gangsterism and kingship over a trailer park pyramid. How would Drew understand any of that? Long could hear Kang-Dae's voice—could feel its vibration in his ear drum. The man could fill the air with that voice, its threats and insults. "Everyone you love." How he stood so close you could smell lunch stale on his breath. How he threw his belly around. Drew had never felt Kang-Dae's iron claws around his forearm, the meat of his arms against his back, the weight of him pressing him into linoleum, mouth open and teeth against hard surfaces with the force of a jet plane, no escape, no room to move or breathe, waiting for it to end as Kang-Dae threatened, promised, his voice resonating through your body.

"Mistakes cost more than you think."

Long would not mention the truth of his father's

murder to them again. Their sympathy was painful. He had only needed to get his theory off his chest. He gunned the El Camino at the apex of a turn, like his dad had taught him. Underneath the fresh snow, the tires found black ice. The car spun twice.

From the backseat, Drew prayed aloud. "Save me, Jesus."

Gerry clutched at Long's chest, dug in his nails. "Oh shit, Long!"

Long gasped.

The car slid sideways across a yard, its back bumper crunching against a maple older than their grandparents. The rear windshield shattered over Drew. A lone brown maple leaf, which had clung stubbornly to the tree all winter, floated down, landed on his bleeding forehead.

THE ART OF FORGIVENESS

LONG KEEPS THE GUN in his sock drawer for three years without looking at it. Things come to a head when Drew pops by with news. Newspaper news.

"How's school?" Long asks.

"Eighteen months to go." Drew slams the *Daily News* onto the kitchen table, open to a six-line story on a page near the back. He is always reading the newspaper and going on about the government. It isn't the first time Drew has come by with a newspaper to show Long some story in the *Daily (Crime) News*. Usually it's about some junkie or dealer who got shot. "Who's next, Long? Could be you. Got to pay the piper some time. Don't you think?"

Good motivation for Long to keep his private life private.

This headline is different though. It's about a suicide note. Written by a dead drug dealer, who confessed to murdering a junkie three years earlier, in 1992. The so-called junkie was Long's father. The confessor was a 21-year-old kid from up the road, who actually was a junkie. Kevin Grant. Long knew him well. Liked to play with guns. Before he got busted, he'd been the unreliable right hand and occasional enforcer for Kang-Dae, the trailer park's self-appointed king, the man in charge of illicit goods—from dubbed porno to uppers to fake Tommy Hilfiger. Long had admired Kevin's tough persona, the way he could show a weapon without saying a word, and you knew he'd use it. The newspaper said Kevin murdered his father. Apparently he lived with that secret for three years, until his conscience got the best of him, effectively avenging Long's father. If Long had known Kevin had been the triggerman, he'd have saved his conscience the trouble.

Long pounds on the newspaper, tipping the round kitchen table.

"I thought you'd be happy."

Long kicks the table and goes to his mother's room, then returns to the kitchen. Drew looks at him expectantly. He shakes his head and goes to his own room. His little brother Mateo is there, too engrossed in his video games to pay attention to Long. Long opens his sock drawer and pulls out the gun, shoves it into his pocket. When he turns back, Mateo is staring, his game forgotten. "Go get fucking supper ready. Mummy will be home from work soon. You think she should have to cook after a ten-hour shift? You think you should be the only one who doesn't do any work around here?"

Long goes back to the kitchen, grabs the newspaper, kicks the door open and sprints up the street, Drew trailing behind. He knocks on Kang-Dae's door, only somewhat aware it is strange to knock on the door of a man you intend to kill.

—

Three years earlier, when Long's dad had been killed, rumours ran around school as the cops ran around the trailer park, sometimes camping outside Long's trailer. "Drug dealer's dad killed in a drug deal, like father like son." Drew was over a few times when the cops came by and it was mostly awkward and depressing. Long was a crier, but he was putting on a hard face. The first time Drew was there and they rang the bell, Long told Drew to answer. It was a policewoman in neon yellow-green rain gear despite the sunny fall day. Drew greeted her as his dad would, friendly tone but monosyllabic, as Mateo tore down the hall behind him and into his and his big sister's room. Drew looked back and realized Long and his mom had vacated the kitchen as well.

"Hello," the officer said in the same, chipper tone Drew had used. "Just need to talk to Leonarda, ask a few more questions."

Long had told Drew the first thing they asked his mother was to identify the body. "Identify, like he was trying to sneak into an event or something. Like his body was something they found on some ancient burial ground."

"Did she do it?"

"She threw herself onto his body and screamed and wailed and wouldn't let go. I would have done the same if they'd let me go."

Drew halfway invited the policewoman in, then thought better of it and asked her to wait while he got Leonarda. A second policeman—a burly dude in a puffy sleeveless vest and blue jeans—joined her. The cops told Leonarda they had "just a few more questions" and wanted to check out "just a few things" around the house, take "just one more look" at some letters they had apparently already talked about. They told Drew to go home but Leonarda said no way. Drew wanted to call his dad, who he said would have demanded a warrant or booted the cops' arses back to the donut shop, except really his dad wasn't a fan of Long's family, and had mocked Long's dad's prized El Camino, called it a truck with a hatchback engine. The cops questioned Leonarda in front of Drew, every now and again saying, "We probably should bring you into the station. But you are comfortable here right?"

Going by shows like *Starsky & Hutch* and *Remington Steele*, Drew said he had expected sharp questions about footprints and ballistic trajectory angles and powdery residues, all in an effort to find a devious and least-expected culprit, someone to chase across town in a speedster or muscle car. The questions the police asked were more direct, mundane, and almost sounded like they suspected the family. Moreover, they had asked all the same questions many times already. "What did he do for a living? Were any of his friends involved in crime? Did anyone have any grudges with him?"

As her mother answered, Long's older sister, Angel, sat beside Drew, staring at the television set, which was off. "He kissed me goodbye," she whispered without making eye contact, still staring at the screen. "Right before he went out. He said, 'See ya, sweetie.'"

Drew stuttered a remorseful response.

"He said he wouldn't be late." Her voice caught on a sharp intake of breath. Drew put a hand on her shoulder and rubbed it. She gave no reaction.

"I'm so sorry." Drew snuck away as quietly as he could.

Kang-Dae answers the door with a shit-eating grin. Long jumps to pound the smugness off Kang-Dae's face with the gun, his muscles coursing with adrenaline. The blow sends the 300-pound Kang-Dae reeling backwards, tumbling toothless and bloody into his kitchen table. The table is the most expensive thing Kang-Dae owns, other than his car. It is a big heavy hardwood coffee table. Kang-Dae likes to sit cross-legged and eat off it. Blood runs down his cheek from his temple.

Drew catches up as Long points the gun. "Don't. Long, don't."

Long throws the newspaper at Kang-Dae. It bounces off his face, falls bloodied to the floor. "Daddy had nothing to do with you." He addresses Kang-Dae but he's talking to himself.

Kang-Dae's feet twitch, then his whole body convulses.

"I think you already killed him." Drew's voice is barely a whisper.

Kang-Dae's mouth opens and his tongue sticks out like he's been injected with poison. He starts talking in no recognizable language. "Man tu ta na." He twitches and convulses but the words, whatever they mean, sound crystal clear. It is Kang Dae's voice, but he sounds educated, and ancient. After half a minute, he starts chanting, "Moan tan. Moan tan. Moan tan."

"Jesus Christ let's go," Long says. He turns and bumps into Drew.

"Aren't you going to shoot him?"

It is a strange question coming from the guy who's come to stop Long from doing just that. There will be no revenge. Kang-Dae will live and continue his evil.

Everything Long ever was or might one day have been came together at that moment, standing over Kang-Dae holding a gun. He didn't like any of it. If he could have seen in all those loose possibilities one good thing to be gained from Kang-Dae's death, he would have emptied the gun into him. But there was nothing good in it, not even a moment of satisfaction.

It might have been different if Kang-Dae had been standing tall, denying his role in the death of Long's father. But only a hungry animal would enjoy taking a pound of flesh from a fat quivering heap of it on the floor. Him lying there like that, it could only have worked as a mercy killing.

You can't take mercy on the Voice of God. At that fractured moment, that's what Long knew he was hearing.

"Moan tan," he says to Drew, who paces in a rapid arc around the kitchen table. Long sits on the coach in the adjoining living room with his palms together. Mateo has retreated down the hall to his room, supper unmade. "Moan tan. Sounds like mount-an. Mountain."

"How do you get mountain out of moan tan?"

"They sound almost the same. He was talking in tongues."

"He was having a fucking seizure. Probably dead by now."

"Maybe he was dead then. Maybe that's why the Holy Spirit was in him. Mount-ain."

"It wasn't mountain."

"Like Moses and the ten commandments."

Drew stops pacing. He has a vein visibly pulsing

from his forehead. "You could still be charged for manslaughter or something. We should call my Uncle Creighton. He's RCMP. He could help."

Long has made a lot of mistakes. He has corrupted his friends, classmates, and fellow immigrants. He has sold addictive chemicals. He has thirsted for revenge. But he did not pull the trigger on the Lord. Had Long pulled the trigger, he would have suffered consequences, either of shame and suffering or of terminal guilt. Just like Kevin. All because he tried so hard to be the man everyone wanted him to be: the hero who conquered Canada, made friends, and took care of his family.

Atop the mountain, Long will not need to hide his private self. He will let his true self out, to sin and sin and sin, and he will not care who knows, because Long will forgive others. He will live and let live. This is God's message, via the twitching unconscious body of Kang-Dae. Mount-ain.

"I'm not worried," Long tells Drew. "I am not worried about Kang-Dae, because I already forgive him."

DREW

HOW TO BE KING

AT RECESS, DREW LEANED against the school and watched New Kid, standing alone singing to himself. Actually, there were two new kids. One white, one brown. The brown one was in Drew's class, and introduced himself during attendance with an accent that made Shaughnessy laugh so hard Drew couldn't follow what the kid said. This other new kid, the pale-skinned one, was right in the kick-hockey section of pavement—the school wouldn't allow hockey sticks so the boys kicked a hockey ball toward rocks designated as goal posts. New Kid was about to get run over by twenty Grade 4 boys. Somebody was going to knock New Kid down and stomp on him. For all they knew, New Kid was okay.

The singing was a bad sign, but inconclusive. Drew's parents sang, every time an old tune came on the car radio. They cranked it up and filled the space with nonsense words from ancient songs. "Remember how the way we used to was," stuff like that. They said modern music, like "Wake Me Up Before You Go-Go," was soulless. You couldn't write off Drew's parents based on that alone. Drew happened to enjoy some of their old-days music, especially The Beatles; he was learning "When I'm 64" on his fiddle. Drew's dad was an excellent mechanic; his ma cooked meals that reminded you bad days were temporary. No one in the congregation had raised more money for wells in Africa than Drew's mom. No one had given more hours' labour to the Riverkeepers than Drew's dad.

Drew swaggered to the skinny four-eyed kid, who was wearing a red turtleneck. Another strike against. Kid was oblivious. He kept singing. Sweet little voice, like a girl's. But it was what he was singing that hit Drew. The Beatles. "Fool on the Hill." This kid knew all the words.

"Hey, New Kid. You like the Beatles?"

"Yeah." He broke into a huge grin. No front teeth.

The previous Christmas, the school music teacher had blacked out the Grade 3 class's two front teeth for the Christmas concert. They had sung that song about only wanting "my two front teeth" for Christmas. As if. The black gunk they used looked like licorice and tasted like tar. The parents had enjoyed a good laugh when the kids lisped the words.

This kid was pronouncing the words to "Fool on the Hill" just fine. It made the air less foggy.

"What's funny?" New Kid's grin was gone like that.

Drew chuckled, established his position. Born and raised here, unlike New Kid. New Kid hadn't earned anything. "I love The Beatles, man. I really do." Drew was only exaggerating a little. He hadn't thought anyone else his age was into The Beatles. "But, 'Fool on the Hill?' Their worst song. Don't you think?"

New Kid looked down.

"That pavement doesn't know anything about music."

"I like that song." New Kid's defiance surprised Drew. He already had him figured for someone who would go along with things. "You must not know shit about The Beatles."

"Don't know shit about The Beatles?" New Kid's swear had made Drew swear. Even Shaughnessy didn't swear, unless he was quoting his mom.

"You can't know shit about The Beatles. Otherwise you wouldn't think 'Fool on the Hill' was their worst song."

"Look." Drew was losing patience. Kid was a loser. The kick-hockey boys were approaching. "I don't want to argue. You just got to move."

New Kid hit Drew with a full stare, jaw pulled back. Drew wanted to join the kick-hockey game. Forget this kid. He put a hand on New Kid's shoulder.

New Kid slapped Drew's hand off his shoulder.

"You're probably the kind of idiot who thinks John Lennon's voice is better than Paul McCartney's."

Before Drew could say a word to defend John Lennon's voice, they were surrounded by a swarm of chanting. "Fight! Fight! Fight!"

—

Drew's father once caused a car accident with Drew and his little sister Christine in the car. Their dad was driving them to swimming lessons in town. Christine was in the tadpole tots group. Drew was going for a test to get his elusive red badge. Christine and her tadpole tots were trying to stick their heads underwater without panicking. Dad was running late and told them, almost apologetically, that he got "stuck under a messy hood." He ran an under-the-table mechanic shop from their garage.

Drew's dad made up for squandered time in the usual way, pedal to metal, five-oh engine working hard as he fumbled around at his breast pocket for smokes. Drew was sitting in the front, trying not to think about his swim test, head buried in *Archie Digest*, which was losing its edge. When he looked up, he saw through the rain-splattered windshield that his father was going left through a yellow-turning-red light, heading toward a station wagon in the oncoming lane. Bam. A quiet crunch and jolt. Drew's head snapped forward and back into the seat. A crack in his neck. Dad's hand on his chest. His dad still grey from the grease he'd tried to wash off, face twisted in fear. Smoke billowed over the hood. They looked at each other, then back to Christine. She was in her car seat, strapped in like a glass vase, her perfect self but crying anyway.

Dad was shaking, big fists balled up and ready to raise hell against the chaos. He tried to jump from behind the crumpled door but it was stuck and he kicked at it with both feet until it flew open and half fell off. He ran out screaming at the other driver—a young, Black man with a mustache similar to Drew's dad's—who had come from his car asking if they were alright but started screaming back when he heard certain words uttered. Drew's dad shoved the man a few steps back then came forward with his fists up. Two cops appeared and tackled the other man. Two more cops joined the fray. A fifth pulled Drew's dad back. He raised his hands, showing his palms, breathing slowly.

Drew opened his door, which wasn't damaged. A cop took him aside and helped him unbuckle Christine's car seat, offered them suckers. Christine accepted. It was a cop so it was probably okay. Drew could hear another cop offering his dad a replacement cigarette.

Within a few minutes, the three of them were climbing into the back of a cruiser; the cops would take them home. The mess of the Monte Carlo would follow behind, pulled by a tow truck. The cops had offered to take it to a mechanic, but Drew's dad said he'd rather fix it himself than let some prissy city-hired fruitcake touch it. He didn't mention his unofficial car garage. Drew looked back as they left the scene. Two cops were still talking to the other driver, and another two were talking to a Black woman, who Drew assumed was his passenger.

Drew looked around the playground, feeling frantic, seeing faces of friends, the orange hockey ball rolling away, forgotten. He did not want to fight. New Kid was staring at the pavement again. Drew had no beef with him at all, until New Kid looked up and said, "Fucking Canadians need a real sport!"

Someone was going to pound New Kid for that. Better Drew than Shaughnessy. Drew grabbed him by his turtleneck and pulled him hard. "What do you mean by that?" He gave the warning through gritted teeth.

"In New York we played baseball, which is a real sport. Hockey's for hicks. And by the way, John Lennon sucks!"

The kids surrounding had a good laugh, though most of them hadn't heard of John Lennon before. Lynn Mercer and Charlotte Goodie stood at the back, Lynn twirling her golden curls and Charlotte making faces at Shaughnessy. Stakes were high. Drew cocked his fist. "You have three seconds to take that back. One."

Before he could say "two," New Kid drove his forehead into Drew's nose, dropping him to the concrete. "Fuck you, fatty!" He kicked Drew in the gut.

Drew closed his eyes. He opened them again when he heard laughter. He saw the kid was wearing yellow rubber boots. Humiliating. Drew grabbed New Kid's foot and yanked it from under him. He climbed on, sat on the kid's chest. Drew's nose bled; his head was ringing, his ears thumped. This jerk. The kid did not know his place. Yellow rubber boots. He was not even protecting his face. Drew swung. His fist landed flush on New Kid's cheek. Drew did it again with his left. He found a rhythm and chanted as he pounded.

"Up! Your! Nose! With! A! Rubber! Hose!"

Kids were laughing. Drew was getting his energy back.

New Kid was kneeing his back. With Drew's full weight on his chest he couldn't put much into it. There was blood all over them.

Drew was getting tired. "Say uncle. Admit hockey rules." It was the comments about John Lennon that hurt most.

New Kid's nose bled. Tears streamed from his eyes and mixed with the blood. "Hockey..." He panted. "Sucks."

Drew was going to have to kill this kid. He pulled back his fist, stopped when he heard another new voice, heavily accented, claiming something hilariously absurd. The other new kid, the brown one, was claiming soccer was the most popular sport. Soccer!

The truth about the new kids was that the white one would take a knife and slice a peephole through Drew's blinders, so he could glimpse a fourth dimension, one where papal bulls could be challenged. The kid would bring him to read every book written about the romance of Bonnie and Clyde, and later the recycling of trauma. He would bring him to witness and smell an endangered mainland moose munching wildflowers, and to see a teacher's lips form a cartoon A-WOO-GAH, and to witness Shaughnessy transformed into a bloated pufferfish. Together they would start a private detectives' agency, working to solve the universal mystery of missing socks.

The other new kid would put his foot through that knife slit, and open Drew's mind to the existence of soccer played on pavement—"like kick hockey but with a soccer ball"—and human traffickers, forms of real-life violent familial bonds his parents couldn't have explained or imagined.

These two were not of Drew's world. They made little sense to one who had spent his life in a tight-knit family in North Muskrat, attending an annual family reunion of dozens of cousins and second-cousins and cousins-removed and cousins with completely different names from other provinces and places he knew only by name. But they all stayed in touch. His best friends were two of his first cousins, brothers Blair—one year older—and Scott—one year younger, who romped in the woods and fished and frog hunted and sometimes smashed out the brains of what they caught and other times had mercy and put them in boxes with holes until they suffocated. Blair would never sing "Fool on the Hill." Scott thought soccer balls were for target practice.

There were feral kids in North Muskrat too, like Drew's neighbour, Pete Dobbs, who made up loud raps on the school bus about conversations he overheard. Drew eliminated Pete from best-friend contention when he showed off his panty collection, items stolen from the dresser drawers of cousins and aunts and friends of the family. And there were guys like Shaughnessy and Khrys Smith, who laughed at Drew's jokes and elbowed him in the face in a game of kick hockey. Whatever they had to say, Drew had already heard it.

Not like these new kids. The one with his indecipherable gibberish and long-in-the-back black hockey hair, who looked like he belonged in detention or the trailer park or both, who claimed soccer was the most popular sport, who during roll call called their teacher "sir." And this American, wearing his stained Ralph Lauren sweater and yellow rubber boots, smelling like Drew's ma's Avon trunk, whacko enough to start a fight over Paul McCartney, smart enough to use big words and a lot of dirty ones too, yet too stupid to defer to Drew's natural authority. The truth of these new kids was, they were a savage northbound monsoon that hit Drew at least as hard as he hit them.

—

Drew looked up. He heard, and felt, laughter from New Kid underneath him. Who said that about soccer? Where did that voice come from?

"What did you say?" Shaughnessy was shouting like a deaf old man with a broken hearing aid, tugging at his ear lobe. "I dint unnerstan choo."

Drew climbed off New York, smiling. This was good luck. He could be a spectator now. He gave New York a hand getting up. The crowd parted around the other new kid. He repeated his comment, slowly. He claimed soccer was the most popular sport in the world.

Shaughnessy doubled over, slapping his knee. "Are you stupid?"

"No." The brown kid shook his head, more earnest than New York. "I'm not. You idiot."

Anyone else would have eaten Shaughnessy's fist for that. This kid was cracking Shaughnessy up. Shaughnessy clutched at his gut, gasped for breath. He straightened himself, took a deep breath. "Whooo. Soccer? Nobody plays soccer. Hockey is the most popular sport."

Everybody nodded except the two new kids, one of whom was still covered in blood. Someone laughed, too loudly. The brown kid spoke up. "Here you play hockey. Everywhere else we play soccer. Don't be stupid."

Shaughnessy doubled over every time the kid spoke.

"In America we play baseball and basketball, and football," New York said. "And hockey."

"See? Everywhere plays hockey," Drew said. "Where you from anyway? Don't they have schools there?"

Even New Kid, the first one, laughed.

"My name is Juan-Jaime but I go by Long."

The playground went silent. Was he trying to be funny? Long? Juan-Jaime? Were those names? Sounded like a soap-opera star. Drew stepped toward him, filling a massive hole in the playground. "Okay. Okay. Nice to meet you, Wahai Long a-Lai. But, can't help but notice, you're awfully dirty. Don't you have showers where you're from? Don't they bathe ya there? Bathe you long? By the way, you aren't very tall for a guy who calls himself Long. I think you should have a bath."

Drew spit on Long.

For the second time that morning, Drew took a kick to his gut, this time while standing. Long was short, but his kick had nearly twice the force of New York's. It knocked Drew to the ground. New York cut off Long as he charged after Drew, tackling him at the knees. A cheer arose.

"Get him, New York!"

He got him, wrapping a forearm around Long's throat from behind and squeezing so that Long's face went red.

A duty teacher pulled both kids up by their ears,

bruised and bloody. As she dragged them to the principal's office, Long was gasping.

Drew winked at New York. "McCartney sucks," he mouthed.

HYPOTHERMIA

GERRY'S BEST TRICK: just when Drew wanted to hurt him most, he hurt himself worse, and Drew had to take care of him.

Drew hadn't wanted to drink his dad's rum. Had no desire to be at the all-ages club that night. He'd planned to spend the morning spoiling his body with his mom's bacon and eggs, reading cartoons by the wood stove. Then maybe practice Nirvana on his fiddle through the day. Watch the hockey game at night. But Gerry always got sad around Christmas. When Gerry got sad, he got stupid and dangerous. Drew was the voice of reason through the sad stupidity. They spent the day cross-country skiing down the logging road. When Drew's parents left for bridge at the Campbells, out came the rum. Down their hatches, Gerry from a shot glass and Drew sipping his with Cokes. They zipped on their parkas, Gerry linked arms with Drew—the two of them leaning on one another for support—and pulled him out the door toward the bus stop.

Fifteen minutes into the bus ride Gerry got them kicked off. There was hardly anyone else aboard—a girl their age who had a guitar case and an old woman reading a romance novel through pink sunglasses. The four of them were congregated near the back. Gerry was socially awkward but he liked being near people. He insisted the girl with the guitar play a Beatles song. She refused. He clutched at his hairline. "You don't know any Beatles?"

Drew leaned against the windows.

"I know 'Blackbird.' But you can't play on the bus."

"Oh. *Fuck* that." Gerry waved his hand toward the driver.

"Sorry."

He fished through his jeans pocket and extracted a two-dollar bill. Gerry lived off the 30-bucks-a-month family-allowance cheque, which his father gave him in exchange for making meals and keeping their trailer cleanish. "I'll give you two bucks if you play 'Blackbird.'"

Her eyes went wide. She wore a fuzzy white coat that made her look like a stunned sheep. It was a cold night to be going downtown to play for quarters. She lay down her nylon guitar case, unzipped it to reveal a scuffed acoustic with Airwalk and SkatePro stickers.

"You skate?" Drew said.

She nodded.

Drew put his hand to the back of his head. "I used to but … hurt my neck."

"Bummer," she said.

"Drew tried skating one time," Gerry said. "Couldn't do an Ollie so he quit. 'Ooh, whiplash!' he said."

"Shut up, Gerry! You were too chickenshit to even get on the board." Drew was tempted to remind Gerry that his bad neck was hard earned in two separate car accidents, but he didn't want to whine.

The girl with the guitar had enough drunk talk and hit them with the opening two-string plucking of "Blackbird." As she sang "in the dead of niiiight" Gerry blurted "*Fuck* I wish I had a guitar!"

The woman with the romance novel, who sat in the bench seat across from Gerry, put a crooked finger to her thin, wide lips, her white eyebrow climbing the frame of her glasses. She had set down her book, was trying to hear the song. Guitar Girl was doing a decent Annie Lennox impersonation.

"You can't play guitar, fuckweed," Drew said. Gerry needed reminders of certain things that were obvious to others.

"That's because I don't have a guitar, fungusfuck."

The driver pulled over, popped the rear door. "Out!" They were on the long stretch of endless little somethings adding up to nothing, near a sign reading "a traditional stopping place."

Drew stood, spread his arms for balance, veered quickly toward the exit.

Gerry remained seated, twitched his hands into a gesture of disbelief. "What, us?"

"If you won't get off I'll happily remove you." The driver had a big slab of arm visible, resting on the wheel.

"No Sir," Drew said. "Not needed. We're going. Gone. Going gone. Come on, Gerry, let's get gone."

Gerry stood while keeping his arms spread, palms raised. He looked at Guitar Girl and beckoned with his head. "Let's go then."

"She can stay," the driver said.

Gerry opened his mouth and lifted his arms higher. "She owes me half a song!"

"Come on, Gerry!"

"By Christ." Gerry grabbed his knapsack from the floor. It was full of novels. He took it everywhere. "Girl owes me half a song." She looked out the opposite window. Gerry followed Drew down the stairs.

"You never paid her," Drew said.

They walked to the next stop and checked the schedule. Fifty-eight minutes till the next bus. Gerry kicked the sign post, cursed his foot. "Let's go home. Should be doing university applications."

"I can't go home this drunk; Mom and Dad'll be back by now." Drew thought about suggesting they hoof it back to Gerry's place, maybe an hour's walk, but Gerry didn't like it there. Drew wouldn't have cared but Gerry always got so awkward and silent around his father, like seven years later he was still trying to think of something to talk about other than his mother's death. "There's a Tim Hortons across the road." They nearly tripped over a homeless guy, sprawled across the sidewalk in a sleeping bag. He was wide awake, head sticking out from the bright blue bag.

"Cold night, eh boys?"

"Sorry, sir."

"Cold as wart removal."

"Can I buy you a tea or something?"

Gerry shivered like addiction, pogoed up and down, rubbing his sleeves together. Drew always felt bad for homeless guys. Why not give them a little something? He'd be in a warm bed soon enough. Sometimes Drew had good conversations with people he gave money to. One of them told him cold fusion would exist if not for oil companies and the CIA. Who else would tell him that kind of thing?

Gerry claimed Drew was only contributing to the bums' drug habits.

This man in the blue sleeping bag refused Drew's offer and countered with his own. He pulled an arm from his bag and opened up his hand, revealing two pink pills the size of Aspirin.

"What magic is this?" Gerry asked, halting his jumping and shivering routine.

"Brand new. All the rage in Europe, big-time happy pills. All euphoria, no side effects. Five bucks."

"No side effects? Where'd you get those?"

"Well if you don't want it that's fine with me." The man pulled his arm back inside his sac.

Gerry dug into his pockets and started pulling out quarters.

"You can't be serious," Drew said.

With his two-dollar bill, Gerry had a total of $4.75. "Lend me a quarter?"

Drew took Gerry's money, pulled out a ten, and held it down for their man, who snatched it and pressed both pills into Drew's palm. "You can take these yourself or give'm to some sweet young girlies at the sock-hop. They get real horny."

"Uh-huh," Gerry said. "Gimme."

"Don't you want to give it to a girlie at the sock-hop?" Drew said. "You could use the help."

"I'd still have to talk to her first, don't you think?"

"True. I hope this ain't candy."

"I hope it isn't Javex."

The all-ages club was its usual mix of sticky floors, punks, skater rats, teetotallers and wannabe ravers. Gerry checked his bag and asked Drew about his favourite local band, which one time they caught there on a random Saturday night. Now they were all Gerry thought about. "Fucking tight that band."

"Yeah."

"These chicks are hot." His head bobbed at double the beat put out by the all-girl punk band, four of them cramped together on a corrugated metal stage.

"They're called Jailbait for a reason."

"Really?" Gerry's smile lit up sin like a backwoods bonfire.

"They're like fourteen years old. Introduce yourself. Better hurry, it's almost their bedtime. Their parents will be here to drive them back to Chester."

"Can't believe I couldn't tell." Gerry's shouting turned the heads of punks and geeks down into the pit.

"Careful man, you'll get us stomped." Drew laughed, found he couldn't stop.

Gerry was laughing too. "Hey, can you buy me a Coke, man? I'm parched." He giggled some more.

As he went to get the Cokes, Drew—half amused and half still longing for the wood stove and Hockey Night in Canada—watched Gerry bobbing his head, wearing that face-eating grin. Drew bumped hard into Shelly Ross, from up his street. When she was a kid, Shelly used to try to peel the skin off ants. When the boys played kick hockey in elementary school, she used to watch, and when the ball squirted out of bounds she'd grab it and say, "Oh look, I found an orange," pretend to take a bite from it. She wouldn't give it back unless the boys said, "Miss, have you seen our orange?" She used to inspect people's garbage on the way to the bus stop on garbage day. Drew asked her about it once. "Just making sure everything's in order," she had said. She was an outcast until junior high, when she developed perky breasts on a slim physique. When she went alternative-goth in Grade 9, Drew figured it was to escape unwanted attention.

"Hey Drew." Shelly put both hands on his chest to keep him from ploughing her into the layer of sucrose over the black-and-white tiled floor. The moment she touched him, he forgot all about Don Cherry and the Maple Leafs.

"Hey! Shelly! Wow. So good to see you." He wrapped his arms all the way around her. She was so thin, he could have touched elbows behind her back.

"You too. Wow."

"You look *fantastic*." She wore a tight black turtleneck and black skirt that stopped just above her ankle. Layered uneven-length hair framed her green eyes. Drew didn't normally go for that look. Tonight he was overwhelmed by her perfection—nothing and no one had ever looked better. "*Really* ... um, pretty."

Shelly put a hand back on his chest, lightly, and ran it down toward his belly. "You drunk?" Flirtatious smile.

"Yeah. You?" The entire world depended on him kissing her. Everything in his life had rolled along a logical path to that moment. One all-night-kiss, like in a rock video. Forever they stared at each other, wondering why they'd never done it before in all the years they were practically neighbours. Jailbait finished their set and hurried off the stage, a Dartmouth boy hopped aboard the drum kit to keep the crowd warm. Still they stood at close range, smiling at one another.

They leaned forward, slowly slow. Drew felt the warm boozy taste of her tongue, wrestling frantically with his own. She was a terrible kisser. Too rushed. Didn't matter. Drew didn't feel thirsty anymore.

The Dartmouth drummer made way for a Halifax band—not the one Gerry loved—before Shelly pulled her lips from Drew's, jammed her tongue into his ear. "Bathroom?" She jammed her crotch against his hand.

Drew had heard rumours about people hooking up in the bathrooms. The stall had no door. The toilet overflowed with piss, shit and puke. The walls were covered with cock drawings, pentagons and swastikas. The sinks backed up, spewing greyish water onto the floors, which you had to wade through. Drew couldn't imagine taking a shit there, let alone losing his virginity. He was surprised at the patience of the people waiting to piss while he and Sherry made out. Some waited a while and smiled knowingly, some laughed and pulled their friends over to see, some left and went to use the can at the Subway sandwich shop while Drew and Sherry went at it, groping and feeling each other up and down.

"You're super hot, Drew."

"You too, babe."

"You're like a heater."

She hiked up her skirt and wrapped her thin legs around his waist. She grabbed his hand and pulled it onto her bright pink panties. Drew tugged them aside. When she opened her mouth and exhaled a soft, high moan, Drew noticed from the corner of his eye a couple of early teen kids gawking, transfixed.

And he heard his name. "Drew!" The voice fun forgot. "We got to go."

"No." He kissed Sherry, wanting his mouth full, an excuse not to answer Gerry.

"We got to go!"

Gerry squeezed past the gawkers and bladder holders, into the stall. Somebody booed.

"Drew, come on." He put his mouth to Drew's ear while Sherry leaned away, against the filthy wall. "I accidentally elbowed one of those Jailbait chicks in the mosh pit. I think her brother and his friends want to hurt me." Gerry had a supernatural knack. "Sorry. Hi, Sherry."

Drew inhaled, gathering his strength. He eased Sherry's legs down so she could stand. He whispered an apology, turned and left. Straight from the stall, through the club and out to the street.

Gerry followed, his voice in Drew's ear. "Do you think you should have just left her exposed like that?"

"Fuck you, Gerry."

"I couldn't stay there. You left me all alone, man. I was so fucking thirsty."

Drew stopped, Gerry kept going and slammed into him from behind. Drew winced, sucked a hard breath and pivoted to face Gerry. "Did you lie? About those guys wanting to hurt you?"

"I really did elbow that chick. Pretty hard."

"And her brother?"

"No, man. No brother. Actually, she was pretty cool about it. I'm sorry. I was just..."

Drew glared, slow rage enveloping his body.

"I was so restless. Drew. It's almost Christmas." He started crying, a high whine, like a puppy in a cage. "Just me and Dad. Watching Scrooge. Listening to the clock."

The only honest response Drew could think of was to punch Gerry in the face. He put all he had into it. He missed by a few feet.

Gerry didn't flinch. Had no reason to. "I'm very fucking thirsty," he said.

Drew left him that way, thirsty, self-pitying, unrepentant. When he got back inside the club, after a frantic search, he found Sherry standing just offstage, making out with the Dartmouth drummer.

On the street there was no sign of Gerry. Drew called a cab and had the driver circle the block a few times. No Gerry. "Guess he bummed bus fare," Drew said to the driver. The ride home cost him a night's wages at the It Store.

At home, he stumbled through the front door and into his father, who said, "You owe me twenty for the rum."

In the morning a phone call woke him, stiff as carbon, pains shooting through his neck and back, with a terrible headache and dry heaves. Gerry was calling from the Infirmary. "I tried to jog home but, it's a long way, especially carrying my book bag. Guess I didn't make it. Doctors said the booze and that pill thinned my blood. Hypothermia, Drew."

Gerry's best trick.

REALLY KILLING

THE WAY HIS DAD LOOKS in the hospital after his stroke: face red and swollen, highways of tubes jammed between him and the officiously beeping machinery that keeps him alive. His hospital gown hangs open, his curly chest hairs are impossibly white. The doctors and nurses and Drew's sister, Christine who is in veterinary school, all keep saying talk to him. Touch him. It would help. Drew finds a spot on his father's shoulder that is free of tubing, and puts his hand there.

"Hi. Hi there. Dad."

Dad would want Drew to be strong. He'd tell him to be however he wanted to be, to feel what he really felt—he'd say maturity comes when a man can be himself—but actually he'd want Drew to be stronger than Ma or Christine. Christine could be sad or worried, these were natural womanly states, but Drew has to be rock solid, everything under control.

"You're going to be alright, Dad. It's going to take a little time, is all."

A nurse comes by and replaces a drip. What would Dad think if he knew a male, Indian nurse was watching his vital signs? His father's chin looks enormous, Leno-like, swollen. It juts up, a look-off point providing a vista of his bushy eyebrows. Other than that, he is all long lines etched in pale skin. New wrinkles.

These are things Drew looks at, instead of the trach tube strapped around his father's throat, instead of the machine violently shoving intermittent bursts of air into his lungs. Dad is in and out of consciousness. He needs the breathing machine for parts of the day. Drew isn't clear on what caused that. Christine's explanation goes over his head, or through his ears. Mr. Casey is on the mend, the medical staff say. That is the main thing. Drew has come at a bad time. He shouldn't have put it off this long. His father is exhausted from passive physio, when they move his limbs around to keep them from atrophying. He is sleeping, so Drew stands and stares, gets to know Dad's face in a way he hasn't been comfortable doing before.

Drew doesn't know what to say. Dad usually leads their sporadic conversations, or monopolizes them. Since Drew was a boy, his father has always been more an advice dispenser than a fully realized person. Not much has changed since Drew moved out and got a real job. When Drew speaks to his father, it is usually to thank him, or dispute whatever wisdom he's just provided or, occasionally, argue about music, politics, or sports.

Drew first started doubting his father's authority around the time of the provincial Scout Truck Rally. Drew's Scout leader specifically stated that "each truck must be designed and built by the Scout." All he gave them was a baggie with a block of wood, four plastic wheels and four thin nails. "You're a really resourceful kid," he said when he gave Drew his kit. He winked as he said it. "See if you can come up with a winner for provincials."

Drew took it home and, looking at his father's 62 Austin Healey poster in the garage, sketched out the most bad-ass, yet classic, looking pinewood racer ever conceived. He showed it to his dad, who took a corner of Drew's blueprint between finger and thumb, a plume of smoke billowing from his cigarette as he sharply exhaled a plume. "Too much goddamn friction. Way too front heavy. Gimme them screws."

Drew obeyed, stomach weighted with what he'd just initiated. First, his dad would be full of suggestions, downright euphoric at the prospect of mentoring his only son. Drew would follow along, even letting the old man take over a little, excited to try out his suggestions, maybe win one for the Scout troop. But Drew would screw it up somehow. Dad would lose interest. He had been a Scout leader Drew's first year. He quit when he learned they couldn't hunt—not even the leaders. When Drew wanted fiddle lessons, their priest offered to lend him an old fiddle. Dad refused, took him shopping for his own. Drew got busy playing pickup football that summer, nearly every night with friends, and didn't practice the fiddle. Dad confiscated it, hid it somewhere in his room for a month and after he gave it back he complained about the noise every time Drew played.

Drew tried to swallow his dread as Dad clamped the nails into his drill press and sanded them down. "Can I try?" His voice sounded squeaky. Dad grunted, put out his smoke, duct-taped the drill trigger down and let his son have a go. Now Drew was smiling, working with his fingers as his dad grunted. "Careful. Careful there." Drew filed for a while and Dad took a look. He nodded his approval then touched them up anyway, doused them in some chemical compound and stuck them through the plastic wheels.

"Finish this tonight."

"Can I help though?"

"Do your homework first. If there's anything left to do then you can help. The principle's simple: keep the weight near the back to give you maximum thrust at the bottom of the track. Reduce friction as much as possible—that's why we'll bend the axels a couple degrees, throw some graphite on the wheels. And keep it fairly aerodynamic. You're probably learning this in science class." Dad always figured Drew for about five grades more advanced than he was. "The rest is grip n' rip."

Drew nodded, loving what his father was telling

him, hating that he wouldn't be allowed to do it himself, loving the smell of grease, tobacco, coffee, and rum that was Dad's garage. He was done his workday, so he wore cargo shorts and a white (but yet, mostly black) tank-top undershirt.

"What's grip n' rip?"

Dad looked offended. He held his thumb and forefinger up. "Hold it," he said. "At the top of the track. Then let go."

Drew rushed through his homework and ran back. Dad let him watch for a few minutes, until Ma called out to him asking if he had finished his research paper on Scottish settlers, which was due in the morning. Drew hadn't started. He hit the *Funk & Wagnalls*, which didn't have much on Nova Scotia, and called his granny, who didn't know or think much about the Scots, and he called his cousin Joannie, who gave Drew the rundown on what she wrote when she did the same paper the previous year. She also gave him some Scout-truck racing tips. She said to have one of the front wheels slightly raised to ride the middle rail. Drew didn't know how she knew these things, but she had the inside scoop on everything.

Dad hated the idea. "Ridiculous. Joannie. Like we take mechanical advice from Joannie."

"She's pretty smart."

"Book smart."

"You say I'm book smart."

"You are. But you can shoot a deer. It's late. I'll take

care of this. Don't worry, bud."

Drew usually let that kind of thing go, but it nagged at him for nearly an hour before he called Joannie back, looking for a better argument. The gist of it was, "The winners all do it."

Which Drew did tell Dad. At which point, Dad dropped his drill and told Drew to do it his fucking self then, but don't touch the fucking tools. Drew touched one. A hammer. He clenched his first around it, raised it over the drill and held it aloft until his fist shook like a badly designed Scout truck. Drew wanted to build it on his own, but Dad would come and watch him lose and say, "Well that was that then."

Fuck that. Drew took the hammer and smashed the shit out of the Scout truck. He picked up the pulp and shoved it back in its little baggie, brought it to Dad as he sat in his recliner watching a sitcom, and dropped the baggie in his lap.

Dad didn't say a word, didn't flinch. Reached into his pocket and pulled out a smoke.

Ma retrieved Drew from his room, where he was putting the flourishing touches on an essay called "If It's Not Irish, It's Nova Scotia!" She pinched Drew by the flab of his elbow and dragged him down to apologize to Dad, under the threat of her doing his Sega like he did his Scout truck. She stood there counting, waiting for it, like Drew was still that seven-year-old boy who shoved his sister's head underwater and wouldn't let her up. Drew said the sorry and Ma was satisfied.

Dad shook his head and looked at the television. "Something's just off. Total fruitcake."

There's a chair next to his father's hospital bed and for several minutes, maybe thirty, he sits, trying to think of something worth saying, but he falls back on his usual. "Habs are doing better since the new year," Drew says, which for some reason reminds him to say it is storming outside, the biggest one of the year, and the forecast calls for several days of it. "Least you don't have to shovel." Drew forces a laugh and remembers his dad recently bought himself a 76-centimetre heavy-condition Husqvarna snow thrower. Drew promises to do the driveway and check the oil too. He sits on a stool by the bed, pulls a Hot Rod meat stick from his pocket, bites at the wrapper to rip it open, pulls it from his mouth, and lets it dangle under his lips.

"So." He speaks into the Hot Road like a microphone. "I decided to go across Canada on the train, see my country: the great Rockies, the vast prairies, the big T-O, the pickup trucks in northern Ontario." He pauses. It's important to pause and leave space for the audience to laugh. "Being from the Maritimes, I decided to start in Toronto. That's a little Newfoundland logic for you."

Pause.

"Yeah, I'd seen every pub in the Maritimes and every strip joint in Montreal. Naw, I'm kidding. That would be a full-time occupation wouldn't it? I'd have to give up watching television, spend no more than five minutes at each strip joint, travelling from club to club for eight hours a day, for about, say, fifty-five years ... Hey, wait, there may be something to this."

He feels flaws throughout his delivery. The wording is awkward. Some of the jokes are plain, or nonsensical, and he's uncertain the payoff is worth the buildup. It's probably too much material for five minutes. "Do I sound natural, Dad? At all?"

Dad is noncommittal.

A few months ago Drew started performing standup comedy for his dog. Actually the thing started when he was alone at work, doing a small job on a rickety, steep, rusted fire escape, his back convex around a metal pole digging in just over his glutes, hanging fifty feet above a parking lot. The upper half of his body was contorted so he could look up from the frozen metal platform to see his target. His hips twisted like a trick rider and every extremity was numb before he started the weld. The men he usually worked with, they were as crooked and hardened as he expected to become. He already had the neck pain and the gut and the reliance on four-letter words. As he worked, he thought about how shitty it would be for the people in the building if they ever had to use that fire escape, how death is the great trickster, that inevitable ending no one sees coming even as it steams straight toward us for decades. What would these low-rise dwellers leave behind? More than Drew would. Families, at least. Children to carry their names, genes, tics and idiosyncrasies. Echoes of their own existence. He had worked on some bridges, one looking exactly like the next, and he made them safer than they had been. Extending a few human lives, that was his legacy. No one could see it though, not even the survivors.

He cared more that he'd made some people laugh. That made him feel like a birthday cake sparkler, when someone laughed at a wiseass comment or something a little too blue for the workplace. He'd once been called, without a trace of irony, "the funniest goddamn welder east of Montreal." That could be his epitaph, he supposed. Better than "saved the lives of the oblivious."

He spent the rest of his afternoon labours conjuring one liners, his mind somehow in two places at once. He was eager to try these jokes out loud, but afraid they wouldn't land, that they'd be met with awkward silence. Maybe it was easier to make people laugh in the moment, during the easy exchange of quips with the fellas, than it was to pre-plan funniness.

When he came home at suppertime his dog, Shannon, ran from his bedroom and jumped into his arms, barking and licking. She was no more than 15 pounds, a border terrier, but she put a jolt into Drew. He figured her to be a safe audience. She wouldn't laugh but her silence wouldn't be an insult. After he'd eaten its contents, he held up a hearty-Irish-stew can and had her sit. She whimpered and stared at the can, twitching her tail, her behind following it, side to side.

"How about a joke, darling? If it's funny, you can have the leftovers.

"Here goes: If I lose fifteen more pounds by Christmas I'll have reached my goal, which was to lose ten pounds by Christmas."

Shannon rolled onto her back, paws up, her whimpers intensifying.

"Was it a good one?"

She leaned her upper body forward and licked herself until she sneezed.

"Are you a dog or a cat?" He scratched her behind the ear. "You're right. The joke was shit."

She gave her most piteous whine.

"Shut up, Shannon."

He put the can on the kitchen floor and she went after it, jamming her snout inside. He felt sorry enough for himself—sad-sack twenty-something bored working a Joe Job his father had gotten him—without a cattish dog's pity. Drew got a sudden strong urge to get his Christmas plans settled. He could probably get a couple of extra days off and spend it with his parents. His dad would have a project they could work on together, maybe thinning the spruce. He might not have split all the winter wood yet. He'd been slowing a little. They could set some traps and try to get a rabbit. They hadn't gone hunting at all that fall.

When Ma answered the phone, Shannon went full dingo, chasing her tail, barking and snapping at her ass, ecstatic for the voice of the lady who often brought her bacon. "Is that my little Del Shannon?"

"Hey Ma. What are we doing for Christmas?"

"Same as always, but I don't know how we'll manage without your sister."

"Me and Dad could cut a nice big tree and bring it in here, do it at my place this year."

"You don't have a tree yet?"

"It's still November."

"Your place is too small."

Shannon licked the phone and Drew. "Okay. Your place then. It'll be fun. Ma? Can I ask you a question? Okay? Don't tell Dad. I'm thinking of, like maybe, maybe leaving my job. Maybe do something a little more creative."

His mother's silence was an act of great patience, a genius-in-simplicity trap. Her closed-mouth discipline spun his molecules so his internal organs slammed against his skin. You can't counter that kind of quiet with your own. You have to announce, confess, lay down your burden, unleash horrible secrets you instinctively want to hide. He hadn't planned on mentioning quitting his job, or trying standup comedy; he wasn't even sure whether he was serious or just dizzy from workplace chemicals and hanging on a suspect fire escape. But she'd whiffed something through the phone. The more he said, the thicker her silence. Nonsense spilled from his mouth. He'd been joking, his boss was hard on him maybe because of the way he'd gotten the job and he'd always been grateful to his father for pulling those strings but guilty that he hadn't gotten a job on his own merits. Shannon kept licking the phone.

"Ma, could you please say something?"

If she were in the room with him, he knew she'd rub his back and say he was a good young man and she was proud of him. It was a mistake, telling her anything. He hung up and hit the shower. Somewhere between rinse and repeat, he developed a new comedic voice for himself. His mind wandered and he remembered from college days when he took the train up to Truro a few times to break his routine. One time there were two greasy travelling hippies making out, no concern for all the commuting suits and certainly no concern for Drew.

"What is it about the train that makes people so horny?"

Starting with a question seemed too Seinfeld.

"I took the train across Canada one time."

Yeah, tell a story.

"It seemed like at every stop, the couple across from me with their tongues down each other's throats was replaced by another couple, also with their tongues down each other's throats, like they were stuck!"

Then the question.

"Why do people do that in public? It's disgusting! I spent the trip afraid to look across the aisle. It got so I couldn't turn my head to the right. I forgot how. Later when I finally got a car, the lane changes were murder."

Hm.

"But, given that everyone on the train seemed so horny, I made sure on the way home to sit next to the cutest girl. And, of course, I made sure she was on my left."

Drew hopped from the shower and found Shannon asleep in his bed. She had a habit of crawling under the bedspread and sticking her head out like a human. He barked her name and she barked back. He launched into the train stuff. "So, I decided to take a trip you know, get away from it all, the hustle and bustle of my life watching television full time. Oh yeah, the soap operas were getting too stressful. When Sharon slept with Nick pretending she was actually Grace? Whoa shit!"

Shannon barked.

"Why are only the women laughing? You guys don't watch? Ohhh no, of course you don't. Me neither. That shit's for pussies."

Shannon looked at Drew like she was waiting for more. He suspected it might be good, or potentially good, with a little polish. He wasn't sure. Maybe he shouldn't say "pussies."

Drew spent hours in his room, watching himself tell stories about a train trip across Canada that had never happened, seeing the way his hands and body moved, eliminating the words that tripped up his tongue. The work scared him, made him wonder if professional standup—putting aside the after parties, drugs and limitless oral sex—was about the same as professional welding: a formula one followed over and over and over again, making sure every step was exactly the same as it always had been. He froze at that thought, dryness in the back of his throat, imagining a conversation he might have with a reporter one day explaining that his meteoric rise had been fairly formulaic, hence the box-office failure of his biopic.

Shannon came sniffing closer, hoping for kindness. Drew scratched her belly. "You know, Shan, the best thing about my job is making the guys laugh."

If a beginner routine was five minutes, Drew's new train-trip material could give him several routines. He convinced himself the material was better than half the stuff the regulars at Yuk Yuks amateur night did. He went there fairly often. Thought about signing up a thousand times, and came close to making it official just once. Almost all of the amateurs bombed. The sort-of funny ones were the ones who were there every week, hoping to be discovered. A lot of them were going for too-soon material about 9/11, only three months removed from tragic horror live on daytime television. No one had any interest in laughing about it. The better ones asked questions: "Did you ever notice...?" to draw the folks in. Seinfeld knew what he was doing.

There was a girl there, a regular who Drew doubted was of legal age, who was at times hilarious and at other times painfully awkward. She wore a bright pink cheerleader's outfit and black lipstick, eyeliner, and nail polish. Her voice sounded like a hundred cigarettes a day, but she twirled her hair and ended every statement with a question mark so she sounded like an airhead. That was her shtick. It worked well enough.

She'd start down a depressing road about self-loathing and suicidal thoughts and joke about trying to slice her wrists with a Barbie leg shaver. Darkness and light with a silly twist. The awkward part far outlasted the joke, which was only a few words long, but what hilarious words: Barbie Leg Shaver Suicide. The timing was good and she closed every joke with a weird, shrill-bubbly Pacino knockoff: "Every time I embrace the darkness, the sparkles pull me back in!" It wasn't the best one liner, but it followed every punch line. It tied her act together.

Her joke about using a talking Jesus doll as a vibrator, murmuring smothered love-thy-neighbour parables to her clitoris, fell flat. She recovered saying, "Not funny in Nova Scotia; and not on a Sunday for God's sake."

Then there were the total failures, who either didn't care enough or simply didn't have it. One over-tall skinny albino guy, who went by the hi-larious name of Dandy Derek, read jokes from his notes. When no one laughed, he yelled at the audience that it was just an open mic for fuck sake. He sounded drunk. Surely Drew could come up with better material, and deliver it more smoothly than that.

Drew had once introduced himself to the cheerleader Goth girl, offered to buy her a drink during intermission, but he couldn't remember her name, and she didn't offer it, saying only, "I don't drink."

"Me neither. Except during economic recessions and when I have lots of money."

She stared at Drew and slowly moved her black lips into a slight smile. "Does it make you happy?"

"Only until it makes me sad."

"Maybe I'll have one."

"If you want to be sad, you'll need more than one."

"No, thank you. I'm already there."

She turned her back to Drew and listened to another regular comic, who had half her originality, tell a story about his failed attempt to assemble Ikea furniture. The mistakes he described seemed cartoonish and impossible but the way he described them made him seem like his intelligence was far, far below average, which Drew supposed was his shtick, meaning he was some kind of method comedian who never turned it off until he got home. Or, he was a legitimate idiot. Either way, he wasn't funny; the Goth cheerleader wasn't laughing but she was listening, nodding attentively.

Drew grabbed a beer and drifted toward his seat, lingering as usual around the next week's signup sheet. This time he found his hand shaking above it, pen in hand.

"Go for it dude."

Drew looked back and saw Dandy Derek.

"It's easier than you think."

Drew wrote his name and phone number, or what he thought was his name and phone number. But after Dandy Derek signed up, he extended a giant hand to Drew and said, "Pleased to meet you Ronnie. Break a leg next week."

When Dandy Derek left, Drew looked down and smiled at what he'd written. Ms. Ronnie Lawrence. The drag character he used to do in high school to make his friends laugh: "Not just the names of the last two guys I blew." Haha, oh boy, like seeing an old friend. Next to the name were a series of wavy lines, an illegible series of numbers. Drew downed his beer and headed to the coat check.

The woman who ran the thing figured out Drew's nervous chicken scratch by dogged trial-and-error and called him to confirm his participation. "Sorry to bother you, but I'm looking for a Ms. Ronnie Lawrence," she said. "I have a number here for her, but it's hard to read. This is the fourth number I've tried."

Drew told her it was the wrong number, hung up, felt uneasy, checked his call display and called her back. He told her he'd be performing as Drew Casey. But his dad asked him to help him rebuild an engine the night of his scheduled open-mic comedy debut. He couldn't say no.

Would it be different if Dad were awake? Still in a hospital bed, still not talking, but conscious? Of course it would. Even if his father stayed silent, there's no way Drew would be showing him a comedy routine. Probably he wouldn't have said a word, certainly not the ones he improvises now:

"My father is so proud of me. Some other father might tell his son not to quit his unionized job to become a comedian. But not my dad. No sir. Not for all the vintage cars in Beverly Hills would my father say that. No, you know what he did when he found out? Hug me? No. Not exactly. Not that. Not that at all. But, that guy is so supportive, rather than tell me not to quit my unionized job? He literally had a stroke when my mother finally told him. That's how far he went to avoid that awkward conversation on my behalf. True story."

It is here Drew commits the cardinal comedic sin. He laughs at his own joke. He doesn't usually do that. He is a deadpan man all the way. But laughter spits through his nose, unexpected and airy. Drew notices that Dad is holding his hand, the comfort of it first, then the age of the thing. Drew isn't sure how long it has been there. For a moment, he thinks Dad must have woken, that Drew's routine has reached into his subconscious brain and pulled him back, more fully realized than Drew had known him to be.

But Dad's eyes remain shut. Drew is the one holding his father's hand, not the other way around. It is limp and weak, significantly softened. Drew hasn't held it before, but surely it was more leathery, hardened, like his own.

—

On each subsequent visit, Dad looks a little better. His face becomes mysteriously beautiful after they remove the tubes. It seems so clean Drew wonders who shaved and washed him. The male nurse? His chin looks more normal.

On one visit, when Drew leans against the bed rail and puts a palm on his father's cheek, his eyes fly open. "Drew." A wheeze.

"Dad." Drew takes his hand away. He imagines welcoming Dad back. In his head it sounds cheesy, so he keeps it to himself. "I split the wood. Since you were, y'know … too lazy."

Dad smiles.

Drew smiles back. Smile like that, he knows. He really killed.

Acknowledgements

These stories took their current shape over many years and iterations. "Safe as Houses" was previously published by the *Ex-Puritan.* "Operation Niblet" appeared in two collections published by Pottersfield Press, including my own *Boy With A Problem.* I am grateful for all the editors' and publishers' skill and work in helping me polish those.

Thank you also to Corey McCreery, David Huebert, Martyn Iannece, Elizabeth Peirce, Steve Law, Michelle Gabata, Dina Desveaux, Miia Suokonautio, Jenni Blackmore, Simon Vigneault, Laura Burke, Richard Levangie—everyone who looked at some version of these stories and helped me turn them into something better.

Chris Benjamin is the author of five previous books including his recent hitchhiking memoir, *Chasing Paradise: A hitchhiker's search for home in a world at war with itself.* His earlier short-story collection, *Boy With A Problem*, was shortlisted for the Alistair MacLeod Prize for Short Fiction. He is the former editor of *Atlantic Books Today* magazine, and currently works as Senior Energy Coordinator with Ecology Action Centre in Nova Scotia, Canada.